HE FOLDS

Fargo slipped the Colt free of its holster, keeping it pointed beneath the table at the old man. "Put down the peashooter, mister," he said. "Put it down and walk away, or they're going to carry you out of here on a slab."

The old man lunged forward, pointing the derringer at Parker's head. "Shut up, Fargo. I'm getting out of here." He shoved his hostage. "Get going."

"Hold it, mister," Fargo snapped. "Don't make it worse than it already is."

He noted that for a man in a life-threatening situation, Parker seemed calm. *Time for another gamble,* he thought.

The old man turned back to snarl something more and Fargo shouted, "Move, Parker!"

Parker lunged out of the way, and Fargo cut loose with the Colt. The slugs took the old man in the knees, and he screamed as he fell.

Fargo jumped to his feet and aimed the Colt at the prone man, who was moaning and clutching at his legs. He put a boot down on the derringer. "See there," Fargo said, after the shouting had died down. "I guess the kid was right. Sooner or later, everyone lays down. Guess it was your turn."

THE
TRAILSMAN

#319

LOUISIANA
LAYDOWN

by

Jon Sharpe

A SIGNET BOOK

SIGNET
Published by New American Library, a division of
Penguin Group (USA) Inc., 375 Hudson Street,
New York, New York 10014, USA
Penguin Group (Canada), 90 Eglinton Avenue East, Suite 700, Toronto,
Ontario M4P 2Y3, Canada (a division of Pearson Penguin Canada Inc.)
Penguin Books Ltd., 80 Strand, London WC2R 0RL, England
Penguin Ireland, 25 St. Stephen's Green, Dublin 2,
Ireland (a division of Penguin Books Ltd.)
Penguin Group (Australia), 250 Camberwell Road, Camberwell, Victoria 3124,
Australia (a division of Pearson Australia Group Pty. Ltd.)
Penguin Books India Pvt. Ltd., 11 Community Centre, Panchsheel Park,
New Delhi - 110 017, India
Penguin Group (NZ), 67 Apollo Drive, Rosedale, North Shore 0632,
New Zealand (a division of Pearson New Zealand Ltd.)
Penguin Books (South Africa) (Pty.) Ltd., 24 Sturdee Avenue,
Rosebank, Johannesburg 2196, South Africa

Penguin Books Ltd., Registered Offices:
80 Strand, London WC2R 0RL, England

First published by Signet, an imprint of New American Library,
a division of Penguin Group (USA) Inc.

First Printing, May 2008
10 9 8 7 6 5 4 3 2 1

The first chapter of this book previously appeared in *Nevada Nemesis*, the
three hundred eighteenth volume in this series.

Copyright © Penguin Group (USA) Inc., 2008
All rights reserved

 REGISTERED TRADEMARK—MARCA REGISTRADA

Printed in the United States of America

PUBLISHER'S NOTE
This is a work of fiction. Names, characters, places, and incidents either are
the product of the author's imagination or are used fictitiously, and any resemblance to actual persons, living or dead, events, or locales is entirely
coincidental.

   The publisher does not have any control over and does not assume any
responsibility for author or third-party Web sites or their content.

If you purchased this book without a cover you should be aware that this
book is stolen property. It was reported as "unsold and destroyed" to the
publisher and neither the author nor the publisher has received any payment
for this "stripped book."

The Trailsman

Beginnings . . . they bend the tree and they mark the man. Skye Fargo was born when he was eighteen. Terror was his midwife, vengeance his first cry. Killing spawned Skye Fargo, ruthless, cold-blooded murder. Out of the acrid smoke of gunpowder still hanging in the air, he rose, cried out a promise never forgotten.

The Trailsman they began to call him all across the West: searcher, scout, hunter, the man who could see where others only looked, his skills for hire but not his soul, the man who lived each day to the fullest, yet trailed each tomorrow. Skye Fargo, the Trailsman, the seeker who could take the wildness of a land and the wanting of a woman and make them his own.

New Orleans, 1860—smiling faces sometimes lie, as the Trailsman learned in a city devoted to lying, larceny, and danger of every kind, including murder.

1

Skye Fargo wrinkled his nose at the stench of the city and ignored the cursing young man stumbling along in the wake of his Ovaro stallion. Squinting his eyes to mere slits to keep out the dust rising into the air, he put his heels to the horse and felt the rope tied to his saddle horn tighten as his prisoner tried to keep up.

Fargo's most recent trail had been a hard one, but the bounty on the man he was bringing in would more than make up for it. Billy "Dynamite" Briggs had robbed his last train, and Fargo suspected that even if he escaped, he wouldn't go very far. Being walked behind a strong horse and a determined man hadn't been good for Billy's constitution—he looked shamed and weak.

The brand-new Minneapolis and St. Louis train company had offered $2,500 to the man who could bring Billy in to stand trial—they wanted him alive—and when Fargo had heard the news, he'd saddled his horse and started tracking. There wasn't much in the West that he hadn't been able to track down and while Billy was a bit more canny and elusive than many others had been, three weeks after he'd started, Fargo found him hiding out in a cave three days north of St. Louis.

Spotting the sign for the train station, Fargo paused and looked back at his prisoner. He *was* alive, but would probably have preferred to be dead. "Almost there, boy," Fargo said. "They might even let you sit down for a spell."

"Go to hell," Billy spat between breaths. "We coulda been partners, split the money and gone our separate ways. The reward isn't worth as much as I offered you."

Fargo laughed coldly. "Nope, it isn't. But that's justice, boy. It doesn't pay as well as crime, but a feller gets to sleep better at night."

"You're no lawman," Billy said, shaking his sweat-soaked, dirty blond hair out of his eyes. His hat was long since gone.

Fargo nodded. "And you're no dangerous criminal, but they'll pay me for you just the same." He spurred the Ovaro once more, forcing Billy to trot in order to keep up.

The noise at the main train station and offices was almost deafening—the M&StL mostly ran cargo, with some passengers, so there was all the racket of crates and cattle being loaded, along with the calls of conductors, families trying to get organized and the general chaos of the other nearby stations adding to the racket. The Ovaro laid his ears back and huffed. Fargo patted him on the neck as he climbed out of the saddle.

"We won't be here long, old boy," he said. "We'll take our reward and be on our way."

He untied the rope from the saddle horn and shortened the length in quick loops. "Come on, Billy," he said. "Let's get it over with." He gave the rope a quick tug and Billy stumbled forward.

"What's keeping you upright, boy?" Fargo asked. "Most men would be on their knees crying for mercy by now."

"Hate," Billy said, spitting into the street. "My mama didn't raise me to be a crybaby, neither. I'll come for you, Fargo, someday when you're sleeping peacefully because you're a law-abiding citizen." He spat again. "What bullshit."

Fargo could feel the waves of hate coming off him and knew the boy meant what he said. If Billy could come after him, he would. He stared hard at the

2

bedraggled-looking boy before him. "You'll want to think might hard on that before you do. The railroad wanted you alive, boy, but if somehow you escape and come after me, you'll only get one thing"—he pulled his Colt smoothly from its holster and placed it directly in Billy's eye—"dead."

He slid the gun back into the holster and said, "Now shut up and move along. St. Louis may be a big city now, but it's still quick with its justice. I'd hate for you to be late to your own hanging." Fargo jerked on the rope and walked up the steps into the train office, pulling Billy along beside him.

The inside of the train office was dusty and hot. The shades were pulled down over the open windows, letting in the noise and the dirt and a humid spring wind, but that was about all. To the left was the ticket window, manned by a balding clerk who looked like he was on the edge of heatstroke, and to the right was a single door marked STATION OFFICE. Fargo knocked on it and when a sharp voice called out, "Enter," he did.

The man sitting behind the desk was hugely fat, with muttonchop whiskers that ran down the sides of his jowls in red wisps. He wore a full suit despite the heat and beads of perspiration lined his forehead. His face was flushed red and Fargo noted the bottle of Old Grand-dad sitting on the desktop. Heat and whiskey weren't a good mix in Fargo's experience.

He glanced at the nameplate on the desk. "You're Mr. Waterstone?"

The man gave Fargo the once-over, taking in his battered trail clothes and unshaven appearance. "I am," he said. "What do you want?"

Fargo gave the rope a quick yank, pulling Billy Briggs into the room. "The reward," he said smoothly. "This is Billy Briggs."

Waterstone's eyes lit up. "That's the best news I've heard all day!" he said. "What's your name, stranger?"

"Fargo," he said. "Skye Fargo." He reached into his coat pocket and pulled out the crumpled flyer, toss-

3

ing it onto Waterstone's desk, then nudged Billy. "Speak up, boy."

"He's right," Billy said. "I'm the one you're looking for."

Waterstone leaned back in his chair, took a long sip from his glass, and bawled, "Jacob! Get in here!"

Fargo listened as the old man from behind the ticket counter woke up from his heat-induced nap and scrambled across the station into the office. "Yes, sir, Mr. Waterstone?"

"Run down to the sheriff's office and bring him. Mr. Fargo here has just brought in a wanted fugitive."

The clerk nodded and headed off at a quick pace, moving his old legs faster than Fargo had imagined possible. He either wanted away from Waterstone, Billy Briggs, the heat, or the boredom, but in any case, he moved fast for an old codger.

"This is just excellent news, Mr. Fargo," Waterstone said. "My employers will be most pleased and so will the sheriff, though I expect that he was hoping to cash in on the reward of two hundred and fifty dollars himself."

Fargo narrowed his eyes at the man. "What did you say?" he asked, his voice like steel.

"I . . . I said the sheriff was probably hoping to cash in on the reward himself."

"I heard that part," Fargo said. "I'm more interested in the amount. Did you say two hundred fifty?"

Waterstone nodded. "Yes, yes," he said. "It's all right here on the poster." He picked up the flyer and waved it in the air.

"Mister, you may think I'm nothing but an illiterate bounty hunter, but you better get your figures right in a hurry. The reward posted by your company was two thousand five hundred dollars, and if you don't have it, then I'm afraid I'll just have to let poor Billy here go." Fargo's voice was calm, but his hand dropped smoothly to the butt of the Colt. "Or I'll have to take it out of you the hard way. Which do you prefer?"

Waterstone paled and quickly grabbed at the flyer, then made a show of looking it over. "Right you are,

Mr. Fargo," he said. "My mistake. It *is* two thousand five hundred. There's no need for threats! The M&StL stands by its promises. Is a company draft acceptable?" He began rummaging through his desk.

Billy laughed. "Fargo, looks like you did a lot of work for damn little pay. You should've accepted my offer."

"Shut up, Billy," Fargo said, giving the rope a yank. He turned his attention back to Waterstone. "Cash," he said to the fat man. "I can wait while you run to the bank."

"I . . . Mr. Fargo, I will have to have the funds wired from Minneapolis. Our operating account here isn't large enough to cover that kind of expense." Waterstone raised his hands. "Please—you'll get your money. It should only take a couple of days at the most."

Fargo scowled at the man. "You know, Mr. Waterstone, when I found Billy here he had a sizable amount of money on him. Money he took from your trains. He even offered me a cut to just let him go." He gave another yank on the rope. "Guess you were right, Billy. Let's go divvy it up."

He turned and started out of the office, while behind him Waterstone let out a yelp. "Please, Mr. Fargo. One day! That's all it will take is one day. I swear."

Fargo looked back at the man. "All right," he said. "One day. I'll even let the sheriff take Billy into custody. But when I come back tomorrow afternoon . . . I expect to be paid. Every penny. If I'm not, things are going to get downright ugly for you. Understood?"

Waterstone nodded. "Yes, sir, Mr. Fargo. You'll get every penny tomorrow afternoon."

Fargo nodded and said, "I better." He turned back to Billy. "Let's go, boy. We'll wait for the sheriff outside."

"You're a fool, Fargo," Billy said. "You ain't going to see one dime."

Fargo laughed. "I wouldn't worry on it too much if I were you, Billy. I'll get what I'm due for the work I've done—I always get paid what I'm due."

Billy looked at the hardened features of the man before him, then said, "I bet you do. But sooner or later, everyone gets shorted; everyone lays down."

"Not me," Fargo said, yanking him onto the board-walk to await the sheriff. "Not ever."

The next afternoon, Waterstone had come through with the money and Fargo had gotten himself some clean clothes, a shave, and a haircut. He'd also taken the time to buy himself a fine steak dinner with a good whiskey and a clean bed to sleep in that night.

He almost felt like a new man—and he didn't want that feeling to end.

There was no pressing reason for him to get back out on the trail, and St. Louis was filled to bursting with people talking about New Orleans and how decadent it had become. Luxurious brothels, expensive gambling, horse racing, duels, and more occurred on a nearly continual basis. For that reason, Fargo decided it might be an interesting place to visit.

Maybe he'd do well gambling and increase the size of his poke and maybe not, but either way, it was someplace new and if he didn't like it, he could always move on. In fact, Fargo knew that eventually he *would* move on—that was his nature—but in the meantime, he had enough money to see at least a glimpse of how the rich city folk lived.

He led the Ovaro down to the docks of the Mississippi River where he booked passage for himself and the horse to New Orleans aboard a riverboat. The ship was good-sized and boasted private cabins and a fine saloon, complete with a fully stocked bar and humidor. Once he'd secured his horse and put his belongings away, Fargo headed for the dining room to wait for the boat to leave in the evening.

He wanted another good meal and perhaps a game of cards before calling it a night.

The waitress—a red-haired wench who clearly had more cleavage than sense, but a nice smile and a firm rear end—took his order and hinted that more services might be available after the boat closed down for the evening.

Fargo grinned and told her he'd keep it in mind, then sipped his whiskey while he waited for his dinner: pot roast with new potatoes, carrots, and cornbread, and apple pie for dessert. For a man who'd lived most of his life on trail rations or worse, it was a damn fine meal and he enjoyed it thoroughly before strolling toward the saloon to see if he could find a good game of poker that would hold his interest.

The main saloon and gambling room was a stark contrast to its cargo hold. Appointed in leather and dark green hues, it encouraged privacy at most of its tables, while the center of the room was dominated by card tables, well lit and attended by serving girls who kept the booze flowing freely.

Fargo wandered around the room, content to watch for a bit until he found a table he liked. Eventually, a seat opened as one man folded his cards in disgust and walked away. "Not my night," he said as he passed by. "Maybe your luck will be better."

"I hope so," Fargo said, sitting down.

The dealer eyed his plain clothing. "The buy in for this table is one hundred dollars, sir," he said. "Perhaps there are other tables that would be more to your liking."

Resisting the urge to punch the pompous ass in the face, Fargo pulled the money out of his vest. "I'm in," he said, keeping his voice even. "And you'd do better not to judge a book by its cover."

"Yes, sir," the dealer said, taking the money and quickly handing Fargo his chips. He glanced around the table once more and added, "The game is five-card draw, nothing wild. Ante is five dollars, no top bet."

Fargo flicked a five-dollar chip forward and studied the other five players as they anted up. Most of the men were nondescript, but there was one who caught his attention immediately. Immaculately dressed and groomed, he appeared to be a city gentleman, with long sideburns and dark brown hair streaked liberally with gray. His suit was pressed and neat, his tie properly done up. *He could be a professional*, Fargo thought.

The dealer pushed out the first set of cards and Fargo glanced at his—a pair of eights, an ace of clubs, and junk.

"Bets, gentlemen?" the dealer said.

Fargo checked first, waiting to see what the other players—especially the potential professional—would do.

Three players folded in a row, then the next one, an old man, said, "I'm in for ten," and put the chips on the table.

The well-dressed man called quietly, placing his chips on the table.

"Mr.—?" the dealer asked.

"Fargo," he replied. "Skye Fargo." He looked once more at the other two players and nodded. "I'm in." He added his own chips to the growing pile.

There was already more money on the table than most cowpunchers would see in six months of work and even though he was flush at the moment, Fargo briefly thought about all the times he hadn't been and wondered if he'd be better off saving his poke for a rainy day than spending it on gambling and booze. Then he grinned to himself. *Better to live well while I can. Hard days will come whether I'm flush or not.*

"Cards, gentlemen?" the dealer asked.

"I'll take two," Fargo said, keeping his eights and his ace. The dealer spun the cards out.

"Three," the old man said, taking his cards.

"I'll stand pat," the well-dressed man said.

The dealer nodded. "Yes, sir, Mr. Parker." He looked at Fargo. "Your bet, sir?"

Fargo wondered if the man was bluffing or had simply been dealt a strong hand. "Check," Fargo said.

"Sir?" the dealer asked the old man.

Watching him, Fargo noticed that the old man's hands were holding his cards tightly, twisting his wrist almost inward. *He's going to bet*, Fargo thought.

"Twenty-five," he said, sliding the chips forward.

It was almost impossible to see, but Fargo had spent many years relying on his instincts and his ability to see what others could not. The *old man* was the professional—a professional cheat. He slipped a card out of his sleeve with one hand, even as he moved his chips forward, using them as a minor distraction.

"I'll see your twenty-five," Mr. Parker said, "and raise you twenty-five." He put his chips forward.

More than anything, Fargo hated a cheat. Poker was a game of skill and chance, but no one had a chance if someone at the table was cheating. Still, other than his own eyes—and he was brand-new at the table— he had no proof.

"Interesting," he said. "It's fifty to me, right?"

"Yes, sir," the dealer said.

Fargo leaned forward, watching the old man intently. People who were flush didn't usually cheat. People who were desperate did. "Let's make it," he said, reaching into his vest, "five hundred dollars." He put the cash on the table.

The old man stared at him, his Adam's apple bobbing as he swallowed hard. "That's a lot of money, mister," he said.

Fargo nodded. "It is," he agreed. "Call, raise, or fold."

"You're bluffing," he said. "I'll allow you to retract the bet. You can't afford to lose that much money."

Fargo grinned. "Maybe," he said. "But I haven't looked at my draw cards yet. And I don't bet unless I'm sure of winning."

His hands trembling, the old man counted his chips. "I can call to . . . one hundred seventy-five," he said. "It's all I've got left."

"Fine," Fargo said. "Make the call."

The old man slid the last of his chips forward, and, once again, took a card from his sleeve. *He must have half a deck up there*, Fargo thought. *He's loaded now.*

The man called Parker sat up a little straighter and glanced at Fargo. "You aren't what you appear to be," he said. "That's a very large bet for a man who hasn't seen his draw cards. Are you trying to force a laydown, sir?"

"No," Fargo said. "But I'm going to make an example of our friend here in just a moment." He gestured at the pile of chips. "Your bet, Mr. Parker," he said.

Parker looked at him intently, then shrugged. "Poker is as much about the players as the cards," he said. "I have a feeling about you." He laid his cards down. "Fold."

"Smart," Fargo said.

"Gentlemen, your cards please," the dealer said.

Fargo showed his pair of eights and his ace.

The cheat grinned and laid down his three jacks and two queens. "Full house, Mr. Fargo," he said. "Let's see your other cards."

Fargo shook his head. "I'd rather see the rest of yours first," he said, lowering his hand down to his Colt.

"I've shown all of mine," the old man said.

"Not those," Fargo replied. "I mean the ones in your sleeve."

"You're accusing me of cheating!" he cried, leaping to his feet. "How dare you!"

"Easy," Fargo said, pointing with his left hand. "Mr. Parker, take a look at the tip of his left sleeve. I believe that this gentleman's luck has just run out."

Parker leaned forward, then suddenly seized the man's arm, yanking out several cards in a flurry. "You are a cheat!" he said.

The old man whipped his right arm forward, a small derringer appearing as if by magic. The room went silent. "Back off, Parker," he said. "At this range, even a derringer can kill you."

Fargo slipped the Colt free of its holster, keeping it pointed beneath the table at the old man. "Put down the peashooter, mister," he said. "Put it down and walk away, or they're going to carry you out of here on a slab."

The old man lunged forward, pointing the little gun at Parker's head. "Shut up, Fargo. I'm getting out of here." He shoved at his hostage. "Get going."

"Hold it, mister," Fargo snapped. "Don't make it worse than it already is."

He noted that for a man in a life-threatening situation, Parker seemed calm. *Time for another gamble*, he thought.

The old man turned back to snarl something more and Fargo shouted, "Move, Parker!"

Parker lunged out of the way, and Fargo cut loose with the Colt. The slugs took the old man in the knees, and he screamed as he fell.

Fargo jumped to his feet and aimed the Colt at the prone man, who was moaning and clutching at his legs. He put a boot down on the derringer. "See there," Fargo said, after the shouting had died down. "I guess the kid was right. Sooner or later, everyone lays down. Guess it was your turn."

Parker got to his feet and nodded at Fargo. "You saved my life, sir," he said. "The least I can do is buy you a drink."

"Why not?" Fargo asked, picking up his draw cards, then tossing them down in disgust. "That hand was terrible anyway."

2

As Fargo and Parker gathered up their scattered chips, two stewards came and physically hauled the wailing card cheat up on deck to await the sheriff, who had already been summoned.

Reloading the Colt, Fargo said, "Let's take a seat over there." He gestured toward a small table near the bar.

"Agreed," Parker said, then turned and led the way.

They arrived at the table and Parker told the waitress to bring a bottle of whiskey and two glasses. The man seemed comfortable to wait in silence, so Fargo kept his peace. After the liquor arrived, they both poured a healthy shot, and Parker raised his glass. "My sincere thanks, Mr. Fargo," he said. "That man was clearly desperate enough to do almost anything."

Fargo nodded and knocked back the bourbon. It was a good label and burned only a little on the way down, leaving his tongue with a charcoal-honey taste he liked. "You're welcome," he said. "Call me Skye or Fargo. I'm not much of a 'mister.' "

Parker laughed, sipping on his own drink. "Fargo, then," he said.

On deck, a loud whistle announced that the boat was leaving and beginning its journey downriver. Both men sat quietly until the hubbub of last-minute noise died down a bit. "So, Fargo," Parker said, "what takes you to New Orleans?"

"A break from the trail, mostly," he replied. "I haven't been there before, so I thought while I was flush, I'd wander down and see what there is to see."

"A great deal, actually," Parker said. "New Orleans is a growing city, and if you've a mind for entertainment—gambling, horse racing, women—all of those and more can be found in the various districts."

Fargo chuckled. "It must be bursting at the seams. I'm not much of a city man—I prefer the open country—but I imagine it's a sight."

"Indeed it is," Parker replied. He took another long sip of his whiskey, then said, "What do you do for a living, Fargo?"

"I've done a lot of things," he replied. "Worked cattle, played lawman in a few small towns when the need was there—whatever needed doing when and where I could make an honest living." Fargo nodded toward the poker table. "I can't stand a dishonest man or a cheat."

"Then perhaps I can interest you in some work while you're seeing the sights," Parker said. "Based on what I saw earlier, you're just the man for the job."

Fargo pondered this a moment. He didn't really need work or money, but if he could earn some extra funds, it couldn't hurt to hear the man out. "I'm not really looking for anything right now," he said. "But what do you have in mind?"

Parker reached into his coat and removed a tattered book, holding it up for Fargo's inspection. "Do you know what this is?" he asked.

Fargo looked at it and shook his head. "Not offhand," he said.

"They call it a 'blue book,'" Parker said. "Ever heard of one?"

"No," he said. "What's a blue book?"

Parker handed it to him. "It's a directory of sorts. A handful of the major cities in the eastern half of the country have them. It tells people where the more worldly entertainments are located."

"Worldly entertainments?" Fargo asked. "You mean whores?"

Parker chuckled. "Yes, though the blue book mostly advertises for the more upscale bordellos."

Fargo shrugged. City people were strange. "What's this got to do with me?" he asked.

"One of the better-known establishments in the city is run by a madam, Hattie Hamilton, who is an acquaintance of mine," Parker said. "I visit her establishment from time to time—it's a fine place—but my main interest is in the poker games held in the private salon."

"And?" Fargo said.

"And," Parker continued, "there is a very high-stakes game this next week. The pot will be worth in excess of fifty thousand dollars."

Fargo whistled. "That's a lot of money."

"Indeed," Parker said. "And that's where you come in, Fargo. I want you to attend the game, watch for any shenanigans like those you noted earlier, and keep the peace. Tempers can flare with that much money on the line."

"I imagine so," he said, considering. "Who all is playing in this game? Not a lot of people—even in a city as large as New Orleans—can have that much money to throw around."

Parker chuckled. "You might be surprised, Fargo, but to answer your question, myself, a couple of very wealthy plantation owners, a saloon owner named Tom Anderson and a man named Richard Beares, who is—like myself—in politics."

"You're a politician?"

"A state senator," Parker said. "So is Beares."

Fargo looked at the man shrewdly. "You didn't make your money in politics," he said. "How'd you get so well-heeled?"

Parker nodded. "You call it as you see it, don't you, Fargo?"

"It's the only way I know how," he said.

"I made most of my money in shipping," he said. "Mostly cotton and other agricultural commodities. Does the job interest you?"

Fargo took another sip of the whiskey. "How long will this game last?" he asked.

14

"One night," Parker said. "Perhaps two at the most. We only have five other players and myself."

"And how much are you going to pay me?"

"That depends," Parker said. "If I lose, I'll pay you one thousand dollars in cash per night. That's a lot of money, I suspect, for someone who has mostly made his living punching cows and chasing down wanted criminals."

"And if you win?" Fargo asked.

"Five thousand dollars," Parker said evenly. "A quite substantial sum of money for someone of your station."

Despite the man's tone, Fargo considered the offer. There was more here than Parker was saying—a lot more, in fact. But the only way he could find out what was really going on was to be there. The other man at their poker game earlier may have been a cheat, but Fargo suspected that the real professional was Parker. He *felt* like a politician, a man who made deals for other people's lives. He wondered if Parker was the sort of man who played by the house rules or played by his own rules. He suspected the latter.

Fargo shook his head. "It's a tempting offer," he said. "But there's more going on here than a simple poker game. What aren't you telling me, Parker?"

Draining his glass, Parker grinned. "You're an observant man, Fargo. I'll grant you that. Of course there's more to this than a simple poker game. No one plays for these kinds of stakes unless there are more significant issues on the table than money." He refilled his glass, considered the amber liquid. "Senator Beares has been moving into territory that doesn't belong to him. He's built himself a little niche empire and I plan to take it from him—starting with this poker game."

"What if he beats you?" Fargo asked.

Parker laughed. "He won't beat me, Fargo. Unless he cheats. And that's why I want you there. The man is a notorious crook."

"And what are you notorious for?"

"Oh, I'm a notorious crook, too," Parker admitted, waving his hand in dismissal. "But the difference, Fargo, is that I treat my people well and play by the rules of our society—even if that society happens to be one that lives beneath the surface of the rest of the country. Do you want the job or not?"

"I'll do the job," Fargo said, "for twenty-five hundred if you lose, up to three nights. If you win, I want ten thousand."

"You're greedy, Fargo. That's an enormous sum of money!"

"For someone like me, yes it is. Enough to start my own ranch or live out my days on a Mexican hacienda if I want to." Fargo shrugged. "But for someone like you—someone willing to risk that much just to put another man in his place—that's not very much money at all, is it?"

Parker looked Fargo over and nodded. "My final offer," he said. "I'll agree to the twenty-five hundred amount, but if I win, you get seventy-five hundred, and not a penny more."

Fargo knew that by negotiating, he'd shown Parker that he wouldn't just do as he was told—though Parker appeared shrewd enough to know that anyway. "Done," Fargo said. "Half of the twenty-five hundred in advance, the balance due when the game is over."

"Agreed," Parker said, reaching into his coat and removing his wallet. He took out a large stack of bills and counted out the sum discreetly, then passed the money to Fargo. "One last thing," he added. "Remember to keep that Colt of yours handy and try not to be distracted by the women of the house. During the game, I'd rather have you thinking with the gun on your belt, and *not* the one in your pants."

"It won't be a problem," Fargo said.

Parker laughed again. "If the look in the eye of that woman who brought us our drinks was any indication, I suspect that despite your appearance, you are something of a ladies' man."

Fargo grinned like a wolf. "I don't object to their company in general, but I like to work one job at a time."

"Good," Parker said. He gestured toward the poker tables. "Should we resume our pursuit of the game?"

Glancing around, Fargo noted that the waitress who'd served him dinner earlier was now standing in the entryway with an all-too-familiar gleam in her eye. "You go ahead," he said. "I have another bit of work today before I can call it a night."

He stood up from the table and headed toward the woman. Behind him, Parker laughed, and said, "Just as I suspected, Fargo. You carry two guns, but it's not the one on your hip that gets the ladies' attention."

Fargo shrugged and kept walking. She hadn't made him wait for his service earlier, so he figured the least he could do was the same.

Her name was Louisa Cantrell, and her voice had a soft Southern lilt that was almost as fetching as her figure. Fargo took her by the arm and they strolled around the deck, admiring the view of the passing shoreline in the moonlight as the riverboat chugged its way downriver. A warm breeze kept the mosquitoes away, and the water smelled of spring greens and copper, like the first minerals in a mountain stream.

"Is it true what the crew is saying?" she asked, when they paused at one point to take in the view.

"I don't know," Fargo said. "What is the crew saying?"

"That you caught a man cheating at cards and shot him twice—once in each knee—beneath the table." She looked him in the eye as she said it, and Fargo admired her grit. There weren't a great many women who could talk about violence and look the man who'd done it in the face. Her eyes were a deep brown, like the heavy stones at the foothills of the Rockies.

He nodded. "Yes, it's true. I hate a cheat."

"You must not have hated him all that much," she said.

"How's that?"

"Otherwise, I think a man like you would have killed him."

"I did worse than kill him," Fargo said. "He won't be walking again anytime soon, and I exposed him as a cheat. He'll have trouble the rest of his days because of it."

"So you think it would have been a mercy to kill him?"

"Sometimes death *is* a mercy," Fargo admitted.

"You are a hard man," she said. She turned to the river, leaning back into him. Her dress exposed the curve of her neck, and the line of her shoulder, white and beautiful in the moonlight. "Do you know what I like about you?" she asked.

"Tell me," he said.

"I like a man with good aim," she said. "With his mind as well as his guns. You don't bandy words and play about like most of the fools I meet on this boat." She turned into his arms, and he met her halfway, wrapping himself around her.

He caught up her hair in his hands, pulling out the pins and letting it fall free. It was longer than he'd thought it would be, full and luxurious. "Do you know what I like about you?" he asked, pulling her closer still, burying his face in her neck and smelling her sweet scent. He felt her jaw muscles clench as he trailed a slow kiss up her neck.

"Tell me," she moaned, under her breath.

"That you know what you want," he said. "And go after it."

He raised his head up and crushed her mouth with a bruising kiss and she moaned again, the sound reverberating off his lips and tongue in a pleasant buzz.

"Do you think your aim is still good, Fargo?" she whispered. "Can you show me?"

"I thought you'd never ask," he said.

They turned away from the rail and began making their way to his small berth. Every few steps or so, they'd stop and kiss once more, their hands seeking frantic purchase to hold themselves upright. She tasted like a fine wine, and she had a nice, mature figure. This wasn't a girl, Fargo knew, but a full-grown woman with an appetite to match his own.

They finally reached his bunk and he shut the door and locked it behind them. She didn't waste any time with more talking, but got right down to business, shoving him down onto the bed as soon as he'd loosened his gun belt and hung it over the hook on the wall.

The berth he'd chosen wasn't fancy—a single bed, a dresser, and a basin to wash up in. She lit the small oil lamp on the dresser top and turned down the wick so the room was bathed in a warm glow that made it appear nicer than it was. Not that it needed much improvement with her in it, Fargo thought.

He watched as she slowly undid the buttons down the front of her dress. She returned his gaze as she went about undressing, moving her fingers without breaking the spell of her eyes. Each wooden button undone came closer to revealing her fine body and as the top half of her dress came free, he felt himself exhale in pleasure at the sight of her full, deep breasts.

She undid several more buttons, then gave a shrug and allowed the dress to drop to the floor where it pooled at her feet. As he'd suspected, she was a mature woman, with a form to match: broad hips, with a slight swell to her belly, and beneath, a dark thatch of curly hair that she kept trimmed and neat. Her legs were long and smooth, and tapered down to her feet, helping accentuate her hourglass shape.

Her breasts swayed slightly as she stepped toward him, the nipples dark and erect points against the fairness of her skin. She leaned down and pulled off his boots one by one, then piece by piece, she undressed the rest of him. This was a woman who knew how to take her time, and she did, finally getting him naked just as he thought he couldn't stand being bound up anymore.

He started to move up, and she placed her hands

19

against his chest and pushed him back down. Her mouth found his, and he tasted her tongue once more even as his hands reached up to cup her breasts and stroke the nipples with his thumbs. She moaned softly, but broke off the kiss and worked her way down, using her lips and tongue until she took his erect manhood in her mouth.

There was nothing tentative about her approach and Fargo felt his hips buck in response to her smooth technique. He tangled his hands in her hair as she worked on him, using her own hands to tease him to an even harder erection.

Finally, he could take no more and lifted her away with a playful growl, then twisted her around so that he could take his turn on top. As she had done, Fargo teased her all the way down, running his teeth and fingers over her nipples, then reaching lower still, finding her center with his fingers. She was warm and wet and more than ready, but he wanted her to ache for him a little, so he continued the slow, torturous play until she was panting beneath him.

"Please, Fargo . . . Oh, God," she whispered. "Don't make me wait any longer. I want you inside me. Now!"

"Let's find out if my aim is still good," he said, sliding into her to the hilt.

She gasped and bucked beneath him, and her moans got loud enough that Fargo figured anyone in the hallway or the berth next door was getting quite an earful. Her legs opened wider, and he obliged the gesture, plunging deeper into her with each thrust.

She was all woman, warm and wet and wanting, and Fargo felt himself beginning to build toward his own climax even as she writhed beneath him. She surged upward, meeting his thrusts with her hips. "Oh, God, Fargo . . . your aim is fine. Don't stop, no matter what. Make me . . . make me . . ." She clawed at his back, raking her nails down, as she screamed, "I'm coming, Fargo! Right now!"

He rode her wave and felt his own climax join hers.

He groaned into her heaving shoulders, feeling her sweat-slicked body trembling beneath his. "Oh, God," she said. "That was better than I expected. You *are* a good shot."

Fargo chuckled and rolled off her, opening the small window to let in some fresh air to mingle pleasantly with the smell of their sex. He lay back down next to her. "Well, I've had some practice," he admitted. "I reckon if more men practiced with a woman like you, they'd be damn fine shots themselves."

She laughed and curled up next to him, still trying to catch her breath.

"I don't think so," she murmured. "I think you're a natural."

"Is that what you think?" he asked.

Louisa nodded against his chest, almost purring. "I do," she said. "But you're probably going to have to prove it to me."

"Prove it to you?" he asked. "This didn't?"

She laughed at the ire in his voice. "Oh, this will do for now," she said. "But it *is* a long ride to New Orleans."

3

The boat arrived in the city of New Orleans at mid-morning. The air was a foul-smelling mix of human waste, trash, swamp, and too many people crammed too close together. In short, it was like most of the bigger cities Fargo had ever been in—no place he'd want to stay for any length of time, and why anyone else would was a mystery to him.

The trip down the Mississippi had been filled with good meals, great sex with the voluptuous Louisa, and good conversations with David Parker, who now stood beside Fargo at the rail, watching as they neared the docks.

"It's good to be home," Parker said. "I enjoy traveling, but my soul belongs to this city."

Sniffing the air with distaste, Fargo said, "That's hard to imagine, given the smell."

Parker laughed. "I'll admit that it does assault the olfactory senses, but you'll get used to it. There are other compensations that more than make up for it not smelling like a bed of roses." His eyes scanned the docks. "There's one now," he added, pointing to a woman descending from a carriage at the far end of the dock. She turned toward them, and Fargo was struck by her handsome features.

She wasn't beautiful in the traditional sense, but her face was striking. She caught sight of Parker standing at the rail and raised her hand in a wave, then moved down the dock to where the passengers would disembark. The riverboat finally moored, and Parker led the way down the gangplank with Fargo close on his heels.

"Hattie," Parker said. "You didn't have to come down here to meet me." He caught her up in his arms and kissed her on the cheek.

"You've been gone almost a month!" the woman exclaimed. "I wasn't going to wait to see you even another minute." She turned her gaze on Fargo, and then he knew why she was running a successful brothel. Her blue eyes screamed seduction. They glowed from within, like a twin set of blue flames, and the passion in them exactly mirrored the intensity and wetness of a woman reaching an orgasm. They were eyes meant for the bedroom, and her smile hinted at every dark desire that could cross a man's mind. Despite the fact that her figure was more matronly than seductive, he guessed that she'd have no trouble bringing most men to their knees within moments. "I see you've brought someone along with you, David. Who's this handsome specimen?"

"Hattie Hamilton, meet Skye Fargo," Parker said. "We met on board during a poker game. Mr. Fargo here has an eye for detail and doesn't take kindly to cheaters."

Fargo took her outstretched hand and almost jumped as a wave of sexual heat passed from her to him. It wasn't just her eyes, he now knew. She was pure sexual ambition in female form—almost a predator. "Miss Hamilton," he said. "It's a . . . unique pleasure to meet you. Mr. Parker speaks highly of your business establishment."

She laughed, low and throaty. "I'm sure he does," she said. "He financed its opening, but he's made his investment back a thousandfold, haven't you, David?"

"Yes, yes, indeed," Parker said. "I thought Mr. Fargo might prove useful in our upcoming poker game. I trust all is prepared."

She nodded, letting her eyes linger on Fargo's a moment more before turning back to her patron. "Yes, everything is ready. The game is set for three nights from now, and everyone has confirmed their attendance."

"That's excellent news, Hattie," Parker said. "I

23

knew I could count on your delicate handling of this. We wouldn't want any interference from those who frown on such high-stakes games."

"Speaking of high stakes," Fargo interrupted, "we probably shouldn't be standing here on the dock talking about this." He jammed a thumb in the direction of the boat. "I'll need to get my horse and my things, arrange for a place to stay."

"Nonsense, Mr. Fargo," Hattie said. "There's plenty of room at my establishment."

Fargo saw Parker's tense look and remembered his earlier words, then ruefully shook his head. "Thank you," he said. "But I suspect I could get a mite distracted staying there and Mr. Parker has hired me to be sharp. You and your ladies could dull any man's senses, I imagine."

She laughed, and the sound was that of a young woman. "Why, Mr. Fargo, I do believe you are flirting with me!"

Fargo grinned and said, "Maybe a little. But the truth is, I'd best get a place to stay that's elsewhere."

"Indeed," Parker said, his voice cold. "Hattie's place is easy enough to find. Once you've stabled your horse, just ask any of the newspaper boys in the city for directions to the Blue Emporium. They'll be able to direct you. Across the street is a decent enough hotel, the Bayou. It's run by a bunch of Cajuns, but it's clean and affordable."

"Sounds fine," Fargo said. "When do you want to meet up again?"

"Three days from now," Parker said. "Be at the Blue Emporium at sundown. The game will begin shortly thereafter."

"I'll be there," Fargo said. "Anything else?"

Parker took Hattie's arm possessively. "Just stay out of trouble, Fargo. This city eats up cowboys and spits them back out as nothing but sackcloth and bones. Be careful."

"Understood," he said. He tipped his hat to Hattie and turned away.

The Ovaro would be restless from several days in the hold and Fargo felt the need to stretch his legs, too.

His horse was led out shortly thereafter, and with a wave to Louisa who was standing on deck and looking forlorn, he tossed his saddle on the Ovaro and began the work of crossing the crowded, dirty city, trying to find somewhere, anywhere, that a man and his horse could feel free.

So this was fabled New Orleans, Fargo thought, as he plied its streets and observed its broad spectrum of the human species. It seemed that on every street corner somebody was peddling something—gadgets or junky tourist mementos or elixirs meant to make you more beautiful or rich or intelligent.

The architecture was more interesting than most of the people. Most of the houses, even the poorer ones, had a certain style that made them worth a serious look. Fargo didn't know anything about architecture but he knew that few cities offered the eye this kind of varied housing. The civic buildings were likewise impressive. For all its flaws, the place obviously had pride and that was reflected in everything from the humblest abode to the gaudiest mansion.

And that was certainly not the only kind of beauty on display. In carriages, buggies, and hansom cabs, and on horseback the range of female good looks was stunning. The rich women in silks, the working girls in scruffy cotton, the imperious ones in gold-trimmed carriages . . . a man didn't know where to look, there were so many attractive women competing for his attention.

Sometimes it was difficult to remember that he was actually trying to find something out . . .

It took two hours of dealing with no small number of rude people with little knowledge of the surrounding country before Fargo finally found someone who gave him directions worth a damn. Following them, he found himself on the outskirts of the city, where swamp hadn't taken over the fertile fields, and the trees looked almost normal, rather than the haunting, moss-covered trees that he'd seen elsewhere.

He gave the Ovaro his head, letting him run. It felt good to be on horseback again, the wind in his face, his hat blown backward. Even the rush of air through his recently trimmed hair made him feel alive and well. He had money—quite a bit of it—and if things went well, he stood to earn a good deal more.

The Ovaro dodged right, around a tree stump, and pulled a tight circle, ready to run across the field again. Fargo pulled him to a halt, letting his big lungs catch up for a minute. Suddenly, the Ovaro snorted a warning and stamped his front hoof. Fargo's hand moved to the butt of his Colt, even as his eyes scanned the shadows beneath the trees for whatever or whoever was there. A faint movement caught his gaze, and with breathtaking speed the Colt cleared the holster and was aimed at the form. "Show yourself!" he barked, his hands rock steady.

"Don't . . . don't shoot me, please," a female voice said. "I didn't mean to startle you or your fine horse."

"Come on out from beneath that tree," Fargo said. "Nice and easy. I'm a mite jumpy, and I've run across far too many women who were good with a gun to go on pure trust these days."

She stepped out from beneath the trees and Fargo felt his jaw unhinge a little bit. She was just about the most breathtaking creature he'd ever laid eyes on. Her skin was the color of coffee with just a bit of fresh cream mixed in and her eyes, large and dark, were mirrored pools deep enough for a man to drown in. Her face was absolutely guileless, unmarked by lies or harsh words, like so many women he'd seen. It almost glowed from within.

She wore a simple dress, cut of one cloth, and her large breasts swelled against the tight, cotton fabric. The ivory color suited her, he thought, as his eyes traveled over her hips and down her shapely legs. From his vantage atop the horse, he could see that she wore no shoes. He holstered the Colt, and tipped his hat. "Ma'am," he said.

She laughed, and it was the sound of an angel singing. "Don't you go calling me that," she said. "I may be a lot of things, but I don't hardly qualify as no lady."

"Reckon I'll give you the benefit of the doubt," Fargo said. "Least until you prove otherwise. You're a long way from anywhere out here."

"I like to come here sometimes," she said. "It's quiet most of the time and no one bothers me."

"I don't suppose," he said. "Why were you hiding under the trees?"

"I . . ." She cast her eyes downward, in the same way he'd seen slaves do. "I didn't mean no harm. I just wanted to watch your horse. I never seen one like that before."

"Yes," he said. "He's a good one. Full of himself, too." He climbed down out of the saddle. "Would you like to ride him?"

She looked startled and held up her hands. "Oh . . . oh, no! I didn't mean that! I just wanted to watch. I . . . I'll leave now and won't trouble you no more." She started to back away.

"Hold on," Fargo said. "You haven't troubled me. I didn't mean to frighten you." He gestured vaguely at the trees. "Are you from around here?" he asked.

She shook her head. "No," she said. "I work in the city most every day. I just come out here once in a while, when I can . . ." She caught her breath, then took what must have seemed to her a daring risk, by adding, "Just so I can *breathe* again."

Fargo chuckled. "I understand," he said. "I don't know much about New Orleans, but it sure is ripe." He took a deep breath, inhaled and exhaled. "It's better out here."

She smiled shyly at him and nodded. "I guess I better be going back," she said. "I don't want Miz Hamilton to get mad at me."

"Miss Hamilton?" Fargo asked. "Hattie Hamilton?"

"Yes," she said. "She runs the Blue Emporium over on Basin Street. Best bang for the buck in all the city."

"You work there?" he asked.

"Yes," she said. "I'm what Miz Hamilton calls a 'special.' Lotsa men like their girls to have some dark in their skin."

Fargo eyed her appreciatively. "I can see why," he said. "I should be the one apologizing—for interrupting your quiet time. I think we both"—he jerked a thumb at the Ovaro, who was busy grazing on the green grass and ignoring them—"just needed to stretch our legs a bit. That riverboat ride from St. Louis was a long one."

The girl nodded as though she'd been on the trip herself several times, though Fargo doubted she'd been more than fifty miles from New Orleans in her entire life. "Do you . . . I don't mean to pry, but do you *know* Miz Hamilton?" she asked.

Fargo nodded. "A little," he said. "We just met today, down on the docks. Her friend Mr. Parker introduced us." The girl shuddered and did her best to hide it, but Fargo's experienced eyes could see that she didn't think much of Parker—or of Hattie Hamilton. "Why do you ask?"

"It ain't none of my business," she said, her voice meek. "You just seemed like you knew her is all."

Suspecting that his earlier thoughts about Parker not telling him everything were accurate, Fargo decided to take the girl into his confidence. "Well, I'll tell you," he said. "Mr. Parker—Senator Parker—strikes me as a dangerous man who likes to get his way. He's asked me to work for him for a few days this week, but maybe I should rethink it a bit. You haven't said as much, but I can tell . . . you don't like him much. Him or Miss Hamilton, do you?"

She stared at him, her dark eyes wide with fear. "No, I like 'em both just fine. Don't say nothing, please."

Fargo placed a gentle hand on her shoulder. "It's all right," he said. "Calm down. I won't be saying a word to either one about you. But I need to know the truth. What am I walking into here?"

She looked at him for a long minute, then sighed and nodded. "Nobody works for Mr. Parker for a few days. It's like . . . like jail, only worse, 'cause you can't ever get out. And Miz Hamilton, she acts all nice and pretty and like a lady, but deep down, under the clothes, she's still just what she was when she first came to New Orleans—a scavenger rat."

She grabbed him by the arm. "You should just run. Don't go back! Head west and don't look back, not even once!"

Fargo gently removed her hand and shook his head. "My name is Skye Fargo," he said. "I've made an agreement with Mr. Parker and I'll hold up my end, but he'll get more than he's bargained for if he tries to double-cross me. That much, I can guarantee you."

She went quiet for a moment, looking him over, like she was examining something of deep interest. "Just be careful," she finally said. "You are going into the snake pit. The whole city ain't nothing but one big den of snakes."

"I'll be careful," Fargo said. He turned back to the Ovaro. "Now, why don't I give you a ride back to the city? I'm headed that way."

Her eyes went wide and she shook her head violently. "Oh, no! If Miz Hamilton saw us, I'd get . . . I'd get in trouble for sure. I'm not supposed to even talk to a man without her permission!"

Fargo felt his jaw clench. If what this girl was saying was true, then he knew exactly the type of place Hattie Hamilton was running. Girls stayed on out of fear of retribution or beatings or worse. He'd seen a few brothels out West run that way, and it was never a pretty sight once you got behind the scenes.

"I'll drop you off when we reach the edge of the city," Fargo said. He climbed into the saddle and reached out a hand. "You've never even been on a horse, have you?"

"No," she said, her eyes darting left and right. "You promise you won't tell?"

"I promise," Fargo said. "And I'm a man who keeps my word."

She grasped his hand and let him pull her up behind him. "It's very high," she said.

Her added weight wouldn't make any difference to the horse on a trip as short as this. The Ovaro had been through far more difficult challenges. "Wrap your arms around my waist," he said. "If you've never ridden a horse, I want you to have the full experience."

"What . . . what do you mean?" she asked, grasping him tightly.

Fargo laughed and put his heels to the horse. The Ovaro responded by leaping into a smooth canter, and turning to take one more run at the open field. "Come on, boy," he called. "Show her what it is to ride!"

Given his head, the Ovaro ran as though he knew he'd be in a stall for a while. Behind Fargo, the girl squealed in delight and held on even tighter. The trees flashed by on either side, blurs of green leaves and the ruddy brown of bark. They reached the end, and Fargo turned him around, heading him back across the field once more.

"Is it always like this?" she called over his shoulder.

"Like what?" he asked.

"Like . . . flying," she said. "So free."

"Always," Fargo said. "Unless someone's chasing you. Then it's a little more tense."

"I've been chased before," she said into his back. "I don't mind that none."

"Were any of them shooting at you, too?" Fargo said, slowing the horse as they found the lane that led back to the city.

She giggled. "No. Why would anyone shoot at me? I ain't nothing but a whore. Not worth the cost of a bullet."

Fargo laughed deeply. "You're mistaken," he said. "I suspect there are plenty of men in the world who would willingly spend the cost of a whole lot of bullets for your company."

"I don't know nothing about that," she said. "Miz Hamilton saves my money for me."

He pulled the horse up sharply, felt her weight lean into him, warm and small. "She what?" he asked.

"Miz Hamilton," the girl repeated. "She saves my money for me. She does for all the girls. We just get ourselves an 'allowance.'"

"How much?" Fargo asked.

"A dollar a week," the girl said, her voice filled with pride. "I save as much as I can."

A normal working girl got a dollar a turn. A beauty like this, maybe as much as ten, Fargo thought. He sincerely doubted Miss Hamilton was saving these girls' earnings. Most likely, she was pocketing the money herself. "I see," he said, his voice tight. "What's your name?"

"Fleur," she said. "I guess it means 'flower.' That's what Miz Hamilton says."

Fargo shook his head, half turning in the saddle so he could make eye contact. "No," he said. "What's your real name?"

"Ain't nobody called me that since my mama died," she said. "But my folks named me Mary."

"All right," he said. "Mary it is, then. At least as far as I'm concerned."

He got the Ovaro moving again, keeping his thoughts to himself. Obviously Parker and Hattie had themselves quite a business going. He wondered about this other fellow, Beares, and thought that looking him up before the big poker game would be a good idea.

Whenever he was in strange country—and there was no doubt that New Orleans was such a place—Fargo liked to know the truth of the land and the people in it. There were always good people in such a place, and bad ones, too. The only question in his mind was who was who, and how to protect himself and those who couldn't protect themselves.

Feeling the warm embrace of Mary in the saddle

behind him, Fargo wondered how long she'd been working for Hattie Hamilton and how many other secrets were being kept behind the walls of the Blue Emporium.

If he were to make a guess, Fargo knew the answer would be a whole lot.

And where there was money and power and secrets, there was always death coming.

In his world, no matter where he was, it just worked out that way.

4

They reached the outskirts of the city and Mary insisted that he let her walk the rest of the way, so he pulled the Ovaro to a halt and gently let her down. Along the way, she'd given him good instructions for reaching both the Blue Emporium and the Bayou Hotel, plus a good livery where he could put his horse and tack at a reasonable price.

"Tell the man that Fleur sent you," she said. "He will take good care of you and your horse. He'll treat you like family."

"And you're sure you'll be all right?" Fargo asked, eyeing the rough-looking surge of humanity that crowded the streets.

"I'll be fine," she said. "Thank you for letting me ride. I won't be forgetting it anytime soon."

"Just keep yourself safe," Fargo said. He tipped his hat to her and rode in the direction she'd told him, feeling like a damn fool. What kind of a man left a beautiful woman like that—even if she was a whore—to walk alone in a city like this? Still, there was nowhere he could really take her, even if she wanted to go.

Despite his misgivings about Hattie and Parker, Mary said that the madam took decent care of the girls. They were fed well, and each had a private room to themselves, and two bathrooms they shared. The customers were usually nice and the Blue Emporium employed several very large, tough men to keep anyone who got rowdy in line. "I got to earn a living somehow," she'd said. "Not too many folks in this city will give work to a girl like me, less it be on her back."

Knowing she spoke the truth didn't make it sting any less. A beautiful woman like that should be cared for, not doing God knows what for a lousy dollar a week. Fargo sighed to himself. If half his instincts about Parker turned out to be true, Mary could prove to be an even more dangerous distraction than Hattie Hamilton.

A woman who knew her own sexual prowess was attractive to a man like him, but there was something even more beguiling in the somehow preserved innocence of a girl like Mary. She'd warned him to pretend he'd never met her if he happened to see her at the Blue Emporium. If it meant keeping her safe, then he'd play along.

The livery she'd sent him to was several blocks from the bordello and the hotel, and as he turned down the street it was on, he saw a large crowd gathered. Everyone was shouting and yelling, and money was changing hands as people bet on whatever event was going on. He urged the Ovaro through the crowd, stepping him up onto a muddied boardwalk at one point, to try to make his way past the mob.

When the crowd finally parted enough to let him through, Fargo pulled up the horse in surprise. Three men were brawling in the middle of the street, though what it really looked like was two men beating the living hell out of one. The two men were older than the third, and each outweighed the younger man by a solid fifty pounds. Given that there was betting going on, he wondered how the young man—really no more than a kid—had gotten himself into this mess.

He leaned down and tapped one of the spectators, a gray-bearded man with a top hat, on the shoulder. "Excuse me," he said, trying to make himself heard. "What's going on here?"

"That young feller is Tommy Anderson Jr. His old man is Tom Anderson—the mayor of Storyville. He comes over this way now and again, has a few beers, talks with folks. A good kid." The man shook his head. "Guess today those two roughing him up kept pushing him, mouthing off about his dad, till the boy couldn't take it no more. It all wound up out here with this crowd betting on the outcome."

The boy, Fargo saw, was giving a pretty good accounting for himself, but for every punch he threw, the other two men landed three or four. It wouldn't be long until they'd pounded him senseless, maybe even killed him. Believing that coincidences happened for a reason, Fargo made a quick decision. "Hey, mister," he said, swinging down out of the saddle. "Hold my horse for five dollars?"

"Sure," the man said, watching with interest as Fargo unbuckled his gunbelt and put it in a saddlebag. "Just be careful in there. Those two men beating on Tommy have got friends in the crowd and none of them play by the rules."

Fargo grinned. "Neither do I," he said.

He started shoving people out of the way, breaking through the crowd just as Tommy went down to his knees. One of the men was shouting at him. "Get up, boy. You ain't gotten half the ass beating you're due."

Stepping into the circle, Fargo said, "I think he's probably had enough, mister. Why don't you and your partner there just move along now?"

"Who the hell are you?" one of the men demanded. "We got us a fight going here."

Fargo chuckled. "This isn't a fight. Two against one and you men outweigh him by a good fifty pounds each. That's not a fight." He let the grin slide off his face, and his eyes turned serious. "On the other hand, if you don't end this right now, you *will* have a fight. The boy has had enough. It's over."

"Go to hell, mister," the man said. He was heavyset and dark haired, with about three or four days of dark stubble on his cheeks. Other than a swelling beneath one eye, he didn't look too much the worse for wear. "Mind your own damn business or we'll give you a taste of the same."

35

"I was hoping you'd say that," Fargo said, striding forward. "It makes everything a lot easier to explain."

The other one—a blond-haired, broad-shouldered man missing one of his front teeth—didn't bother talking. He simply lunged forward, attempting to take Fargo off guard.

Stepping sideways, Fargo brought up his boot and caught the man square in the stomach. The air went out of him with a heavy *whomp*. As he started to go down, Fargo spun and planted a heavy punch right behind the man's ear. He dropped like a sack of oats and didn't get up again.

"That about evens the odds," he said, looking at the other man. "Now, I'm going to ask you one more time to move along."

The man started to say something, but that was all the time Tommy Anderson gave him. In the lull, he'd gotten a chance to catch his breath and get a second wind. He hit the unsuspecting man from behind, driving him to the ground.

Fargo stepped back to watch, wanting to make sure that the other man wasn't going to get up and rejoin the fray. As he'd suspected, one-on-one, the kid was a pretty decent fighter. He watched as the two men squared off, and Tommy snapped several sharp jabs into the man's face, stinging him. He tried to keep his hands up to defend himself, but when that didn't work, he charged Tommy with the roar of a wounded bear.

But Tommy was faster, and sidestepped the rush, snapping out several more punches that staggered his opponent. In another minute, the fight was over, the larger man splayed out on the ground, holding his head and moaning about his missing teeth.

Tommy moved over to where Fargo was standing and nodded. "Thanks, mister," he said. "You saved me for sure."

Fargo peered at the crowd and noticed several of the onlookers were headed their way. "Best save your thanks for later and brace yourself, boy," he said. "Looks like these other fellers want in on the action."

"Damn," he muttered. "I'm already dog tired."

"No time to be tired," Fargo said. He took several steps away from Tommy, making sure he had room to move freely. Two of the men moved toward him, while the third started toward Tommy.

"You shoulda minded your own business, mister," one of them said. "Guess you need a lesson in how this town works."

"I suspect you're about to get an education yourself," Fargo replied.

Just then a shotgun boomed and everyone stopped in their tracks. "That's enough!" a voice shouted.

"Ah, hell, Deputy, we were only—" one of the men began.

"Fixing to get your ass kicked," the deputy replied before stepping out of the crowd. "Buck, the man you were about to tangle with is Skye Fargo, unless my memory has completely gone to hell." He spat into the dirt of the street. "We'd have been picking your sorry carcass up with a shovel."

Fargo grinned, recognizing the man. John H. D. Timmons had been a deputy sheriff in a two-horse Kansas town the Trailsman had passed through some years ago. A local cattleman was causing no end of misery to the town folk and with Fargo's help, things had been set to rights. "Hello, H.D.," he said. "Been a while."

The deputy crossed the space between them, shifting his scattergun to his left hand and holding out his right. "Fargo," he said, grinning. "You've probably been in town less than a day and already you've found trouble."

"It usually finds me," Fargo said. "I don't have to look for it too hard." Both men laughed, then Fargo added, "No, just saw the ruckus and what looked to be a pretty unfair fight under way." He nodded at Tommy. "The boy was on the losing end of a bad situation."

H.D. leaned close and said, "You don't know the half of it." His voice was too quiet to be heard by

37

anyone but Fargo himself. "This city is worse than anything I ever saw or heard tell of out west. Meet me over at the sheriff's office at five and I'll fill you in."

Before Fargo could reply, H.D. turned and looked over the crowd of roughs. "Show's over, folks," he barked. "Move on before I move you along the hard way." He raised his shotgun for emphasis.

The crowd began to disperse, but even still, Fargo saw money changing hands, though whether it was from some new wager on his presence or the outcome of the previous fight, he didn't know. Glancing back at him, H.D. said, "Can you see Tommy home, Fargo? I'd just as soon not have to break up any more of these today."

Fargo nodded. "Yeah, I'll get him there." He turned his attention to the sandy-haired young man in front of him. "How far are we going, boy?"

"The name's Tommy," he said. "Tommy Anderson. I prefer that over 'boy,' though you sure wouldn't know it from what my dad calls me."

Fargo smiled. It seemed to him that almost every young man went through a period where everyone called him "boy," and all that boy wanted to be was a man. "All right," he said. "Tommy it is, until you prove otherwise. I'm Skye Fargo."

Tommy nodded. "Mr. Fargo, thanks again for your help. I bit off more than I could chew, and then some."

"Best thing to do in a case like that is spit 'er back out," Fargo said. "Otherwise, you end up choking on the gristle. How far are we going to get you home?"

"Not far," Tommy said. "My father's saloon is over on Basin Street, just down a couple of blocks. He'll be there."

"Okay," he said. "Let me just get my horse stabled . . ." He turned to look where he'd asked the man to hold his horse and felt his heart sink. The man—and his Ovaro—were gone.

"God*damn*," Fargo cursed. "That sonofabitch stole my horse!"

"You asked a stranger to hold your horse?" Tommy asked, his voice incredulous. "In New Orleans?"

"I offered him five dollars," Fargo said.

Tommy laughed, then spat into the dirt. There was still a little blood in his spit. "Mr. Fargo, your horse and gear would be worth far more than five dollars to even the meanest horse trader in town."

"Yeah, but . . ." Fargo's voice trailed off. He was the Trailsman. He'd find the man—and his horse and gear—if he had to track them all the way to hell itself.

"Tell you what," Tommy said. "You helped me. Now I'll help you. It's the least I can do."

"What do you mean?" Fargo asked.

"Let's get over to my father's place and I'll tell you," Tommy said. "I'll bet you that five dollars we can have your horse and your gear, every last bit of it, back before sundown."

Fargo looked at the young man and saw he was completely serious. He stuck out a hand and as they shook, he said, "Done. And along the way, you can explain to me just what kind of vipers' nest I've landed myself in. This city smells bad and is more dangerous than Dodge, Wichita and Cheyenne combined."

Tommy laughed again. "The West may be rough, Mr. Fargo, but I guarantee you that it's got nothing on the city of New Orleans, least of all this area of town. The locals call it Storyville."

"Storyville? How come?"

"Because of all the places in the city, the best stories come from here. They aren't usually appropriate for kiddies, though."

"I reckon not," Fargo said, his eyes traveling over the rough buildings and dark alleyways filled with trash.

"The West must be better than this place," Tommy said. "At least out there, the bad guys eventually get caught and hung. Here in town we have another name for them."

They started down the street, Fargo's eyes constantly moving for sign of his horse. "Oh, yeah?" he muttered. "What do you call them?"

"Citizens," Tommy said. "The fine citizens of Storyville. And most of them would steal your teeth while you were getting a shave if they thought they could do it."

"What a nice place," Fargo said.

Tommy pointed. "That way," he said. "And no, sir. It's not a nice place at all."

"Then why stay?" he asked. "You're old enough to make your own way in the world."

"True enough," Tommy said. "But out there, I'd be a nobody. Here, at least, I'm kind of a somebody."

"How's that?"

"My father is Tom Anderson, the mayor of Storyville," he said, grinning proudly.

The name meant nothing to Fargo and it must have showed. He shrugged noncommittally.

Tommy just laughed. "Lots of people around here would like to run Storyville, Mr. Fargo. Lots of folks think they do—or will—if they play their cards right. But the real power in this part of the city is my father." He pointed to a corner building with the words ANDERSON'S ANNEX printed in bold on the sign. "You'll see in a minute."

Suddenly, Fargo understood just why Parker and Beares were at odds. Why this whole wretched place felt so tense. Everyone was gearing up for a fight to see who was going to run this part of the city—and get the money and power that came with it.

Parker might have called the game poker, but Fargo knew the stakes were a *lot* higher than he'd suspected.

Tommy's father was seated at a corner table, a potted palm providing extra shadows and allowing him to watch the room almost unobserved. The place called ANDERSON'S ANNEX wasn't luxurious, but it was by far one of the nicer saloons Fargo had ever been in. A mahogany bar ran the length of one entire wall and a massive, gilt-edged mirror backed it.

Bottles of booze—many of which Fargo had never even heard of before—were stacked in tiers, along with numerous types of wine and other spirits. A quick count showed eight different taps for beer, and he detected the smell of steaks and potatoes grilling in the back kitchen.

At the tables, and along the couches lining the walls, women of every size, shape, and color waited to be escorted upstairs. Many of them had coffee-colored skin—some of them were probably mulatto, like Mary, while others were most likely poor Creole girls who didn't have any other way to make a living. These were no backwater whores dressed in cheap clothes and charging a dollar a time. Their gowns alone must have cost a small fortune, and each of them had her hair and makeup done just right. Out here, they were expected to look and act like ladies.

Upstairs, Fargo knew, they were expected to be something else entirely.

Several of them openly beckoned to him or called out greetings as he and Tommy crossed the room. They reached the table, and it didn't take a trained eye to tell that Tommy's father was extremely angry. Not knowing who, precisely, the man was angry with, Fargo decided to keep his peace and see what the man had to say first.

"Sit down, boy," he said. "Are you all right?"

"I'll be fine, sir," Tommy said. "Thanks to—"

"Mr. Skye Fargo," the man said, standing up. "I've heard." He stuck out one large, meaty hand the size of a grizzly's paw and Fargo shook hands with him. The man wasn't much taller than he was, but he was built like a keg of ten-penny nails. On top of that, he was clearly intelligent, with sharp eyes that took him in and assessed him in a glance.

"News must travel fast in these parts, Mr. Anderson," Fargo said. "We came straight here after that little . . . ruckus up the street."

The man laughed and shook his head. "Call me Tom," he said. "Or Mayor, if you like. Everyone around here does. Thanks for helping out my son."

"Then I'm Fargo," he said. "And you're welcome. It wasn't a fair fight."

"They never are around here, Fargo," Tom said. "That's the sorry truth of it. I'm still waiting on word for who those two worked for—Beares or Parker. Maybe both." He tossed his hands up in the air in a futile gesture, then signaled to one of the girls.

She came over and he ordered a pitcher of beer. "I'll be honest with you, Fargo. I'm at my wit's end. Storyville is coming apart at the seams and if something isn't done soon, the whole damn thing is going to come crashing down around us."

Fargo looked at the man sitting across from him, then said, "It doesn't seem like a great place to live. Hell, I haven't been in town six hours and I've already lost everything I own."

"What?"

"Someone stole his horse and his gear, sir," Tommy said. "When he jumped off to help me."

"Bah!" Tom said. He whistled sharply and two men that Fargo, even with his keen eye, hadn't noticed before, came stepping forward out of the shadows beneath the stairs. "What kind of horse?" he asked.

"An Ovaro," Fargo said.

Tom nodded, and when the two men reached the table, he stood up and spoke to them in hushed whispers. They both said, "Yes, sir," then left the bar in a hurry.

"You'll get your horse back, Fargo," Tom said. "And all your gear. It's the least I can do for you lending a hand to the boy."

"*Tommy,*" the boy said.

"I'd be much obliged," Fargo said, "but it's a big city, and I'm sure it's all long gone by now." Mentally, he was damn thankful he kept his money in his belt where it was safe.

The elder Anderson laughed again. "Fargo, there isn't a penny stolen in this parish that I don't know about, nor a secret whispered that I can't ferret out. That's why *I'm* the mayor of Storyville." He slugged back a long pull on his glass of beer, then added, "But I'll be damned if I know how long it's going to last."

There was a man like Anderson in every hamlet, town, and city in the country. The man who ran things. Sometimes he worked behind the scenes; sometimes he worked right out in front as a politician. It didn't matter. He was the man you went to when you needed to navigate the politics of a place. He was the man you went to when you wanted to get rid of an enemy. He was the man you went to when events made you plead for your life. And you crossed him at your peril.

Anderson here didn't try to impress Fargo with his importance. His importance was in the air. Every molecule in Storyville was in his control. Or had been anyway. Fargo sensed that something had gone wrong in Anderson's fiefdom. He sensed not only a slight confusion in the man—Anderson wasn't used to being challenged—he also saw in the gray eyes a real anger. Somebody had crossed him indeed. And whether they knew it or not, they were living at his mercy.

Fargo waited the man out, and after a long minute of silence, Tom said, "If you're half of what old H.D. says, maybe you can help me. Hell, maybe you can save us all."

5

For nearly an hour, Fargo sat and listened while Tom Anderson told the story of his rise to power as the mayor of Storyville. He'd started off with the very saloon they were sitting in, and not long after, he'd added the "lady companions," which seemed like an awful fancy way of saying whores, until Anderson explained that there were many wealthy men and tourists who came to New Orleans every day.

"Some come for business, or the horse races, or even to invest in the riverboat business," Anderson said. "But all of them like to have sex and they'll pay top dollar for the kind of girls I employ."

"So what's gone wrong?" Fargo asked.

Anderson sighed. "Everything," he said. "First, Senator David Parker from Winn Parish—which borders this one—came in here, talking on the one hand about cleaning up the city, making it respectable, while on the other, he was financing places like Hattie Hamilton's Blue Emporium and lining his own pockets at the same time. Then Senator Richard Beares followed suit, bringing our own Catahoula Parish into the fight."

"And the newspapers," Fargo guessed. "Attention you didn't want, but the politicians crave."

Anderson nodded. "Exactly so," he said. "So now there're three of us vying for control of Basin Street, but I don't hang my head in shame when I talk about what I do. I've built most of this area up from nothing. When I first got here, what fire hadn't gutted, the swamp was trying to take back. Now, there are businesses, jobs, trade—it's a real community."

"A real dangerous one," Fargo said. "It's not a pretty place, at least as far as I've seen."

"No, it's not pretty. But it's more than what it was. If those two get their way, all of the brothels will go underground, and the blue book trade will be legally banned. These girls won't be working in a decent place like mine. They'll be on their backs in the alleys, taking whoever will service them for two bits and a bite to eat."

"You don't paint a pretty picture," Fargo said. "But what about the poker game?"

Anderson started in surprise. "How'd you know about . . ." His voice trailed off. "Are you *working* for one of those bastards?"

"I met Parker on the riverboat, coming down from St. Louis," Fargo said. "He told me about the game, offered me a job."

"What kind of a job?" Anderson asked, his voice filled with suspicion.

"Told me he wanted me to keep an eye on things, keep things fair, watch out for cheating, that sort of thing," he said. "He offered a pretty damn good wage, too."

"I just bet he did," Anderson said. "But you can be damn sure that there's something in it for him, if he asked you. David Parker would skin a starving cat for a new pair of gloves if he liked the color of its mangy fur."

"He sort of strikes me that way, too," Fargo said. "But a man in my position can't afford to turn down money like he was offering."

"If you do what he says—keep the game fair—then you'll have earned your wage and then some," Anderson said. "I think the whole thing is some kind of setup. I just haven't figured it out yet."

"What do you mean?"

"Look, David Parker is one smart fella. He likes to gamble—loves it, in fact—but he also likes to win. Out at the racetrack, the odds change when he takes a seat in the clubhouse. This game was his idea. We'd all sit

45

down, play a high-stakes game of poker. The money is part of it, but the real stakes are unspoken. The winner gets Basin Street and Storyville. The losers can find somewhere else to play."

"I figured it was something like that," Fargo said. "The problem is that the whole game has to be rigged. Somehow. Otherwise, Parker wouldn't have suggested it."

"You think he'll cheat?"

Fargo shook his head. "I don't reckon he'll be that obvious about it. There must be something else involved. He likes the odds to favor him."

"Fargo, H.D.'s told me the story about what happened out in Kansas. He says you're the hardest man he's ever met—but you're also fair. Will you help keep the game fair at least?"

"If I spot anyone doing anything out of line," Fargo said, "you can be sure I'll say something. There's more than money or a business on the line here, I think. There's all the folks who live and work in this area. Seems to me like you've tried to do right by them, much as you can. I'm not sure Parker and Beares are so high-minded."

"They aren't," Anderson said. "Ask around and you'll learn the truth."

"I intend to," Fargo said.

He was about to add something more, when Anderson stood. Coming through the door were the two men who'd left earlier, dragging another man between them.

It was the man who'd stolen Fargo's horse.

"Ahhh, if it isn't Slick Willie Smith," Anderson said. "How are you, Willie?"

Willie's eyes were wide and frightened. It didn't look like the men had roughed him up too much, but his coat was torn and his lip was bleeding. "I'm . . . I'm sorry, Mr. Anderson. I didn't know he was a friend of yours! I swear it! I just thought he was passing through!"

"Willie, we've talked about this before, haven't we?

You aren't supposed to be stealing at all. What happened to that job I got you over at the stables?"

"I got drunk," the man said. "Ol' man Simms, he fired me on the spot."

"I would've, too," Anderson said. He looked up at his men. "Did you retrieve Mr. Fargo's belongings?"

One of the men nodded. "Yes, sir. Willie was trying to sell the tack when we caught up with him."

Fargo breathed a sigh of relief. He and the Ovaro had been through a lot together. Losing his tack and gear would be one thing—those were replaceable—but a great horse like the Ovaro would be all but impossible to find again.

"Well, Fargo," Anderson said, "what do you want done with him?"

Willie was all but gibbering now, and Fargo shook his head. "Let him go," he said to the men. They released him and as Willie started to backpedal, Fargo snatched his coat lapels and yanked him forward, lifting him off his feet.

"Don't hurt me, please, mister!" Willie screeched.

"Stealing is a sorry-assed way to make your way in the world, Willie," Fargo said. "Mr. Anderson here gave you a shot at the straight life—got you a job—and you ruined it. Now I'm going to give you one: get sober and get a job. If *I* find out you've been stealing again, from anyone, there won't be a second chance. I'll hang you from the nearest post I can find and spare the world a lot of grief." Fargo shook him until his bones rattled. "You understand me?"

"Yes, sir," Willie said. "Yes, sir, Mr. Fargo. I understand."

Fargo shoved him away. "Now get out of here," he said.

Willie ran for the door and Anderson chuckled. "I thought he was going to wet himself for a minute there."

"So did I," Fargo said. "I'd best get going. I still need to see to my horse and meet up with H.D., and I still haven't gotten a room yet."

"Where did Parker tell you to stay?" Anderson asked.

"The Bayou," he said. "Across from the Blue Emporium."

"I know it," Anderson said. "He owns it, but it's a decent enough place." He looked at Fargo seriously. "This is a dangerous bit of business you're in, Fargo. A lot of money and lives are on the table. Watch your back, and if you run into trouble, come find me. Otherwise, I'll see you at the game and pray that you're as straight an arrow as you seem."

"I'll keep it in mind," Fargo said. "One thing I can tell you: there's only one set of rules I play by, Anderson. Mine. They're harsh but fair. If I catch anyone cheating, you can be sure I'll say something."

"Good enough," he said, offering his hand.

Fargo shook and took his leave, finding his horse tied up outside and all his gear exactly as he'd left it. He pulled his gun belt out of the saddlebag and put it back on.

So far, what he knew was that Parker wasn't telling the whole truth, and Anderson was telling his version of it. And there was still the matter of figuring out what Richard Beares was all about, too.

A lot of people, all of them telling lies of one kind or another.

"It's no wonder they call it Storyville," he said to the Ovaro, who nickered at him in reply. He climbed into the saddle, and turned the horse toward the livery.

The humid air was still and heavy as the early evening sun went down on the water. All the way to the livery, Fargo felt eyes on him and he knew that word had spread.

And that he was being watched by everyone.

John H. D. Timmons had spent most of his forty-two years of life living in bad circumstances and working in worse. His father had been a Baptist minister in New Hampshire who took the sentiment "spare the rod, spoil the child" to heart and regularly beat the young, defenseless John H. D. Timmons within an inch of his life. Believing that women were much like children, the man had treated his wife the same.

The year he was sixteen, H.D.'s father had beaten his mother to death. H.D. returned the favor, burned down the small home and attached church he'd grown up in, and left, heading west and not stopping until he'd reached Oklahoma.

Punching cows was tough, but compared to growing up with the Reverend (as he often thought of his father) it was easy. He learned to ride, shoot, drink, fight, and generally take care of himself. When a group of cattle rustlers began stealing from the Double Bar T ranch, it was H.D. who'd helped the marshal track them down and bring them to justice. From that point on, his future in law enforcement was assured.

He'd worked in a lot of prairie towns, from Oklahoma to Nebraska and then back down to Kansas, which is where Fargo had first met him. The work was hard and dangerous, but H.D. brought perspective to it, wasn't on the take, and treated the citizens who were law-abiding as they deserved to be treated. The years had aged him—he'd gone a little softer around the middle, and there was more gray in his hair than black, but his hands were still rock steady as he poured two shots of sour mash and raised his glass in a toast.

"Here's to still being alive," he said. "And to still being a bit faster than the fella trying to kill you."

Fargo raised his own glass, and added, "Or to just being a bit luckier."

H.D. laughed and both men tossed back the bourbon. "It's good to see you again, Fargo. Last I heard, you were headed to the Dakotas."

Fargo nodded. "I went up there for a spell, but didn't stay. There's too many bad men up that way, stealing land, cattle, and grubbing for gold. Seems like that's all anyone was interested in, so I moved on."

"You run into trouble?" H.D. asked.

"Nothing I couldn't handle," he said. "But it *does* seem to find me wherever I go."

"I'll say," H.D. said. "But it's not trouble that finds you. Not really. It's folks who need help. Trouble of one kind or another usually follows right along with that."

"It does," Fargo agreed. "So tell me straight, H.D., who's really running this town?"

H.D. laughed. "Everyone thinks they are," he said. "But no one really is. The whole city is a mess, always will be, I suspect."

"Why's that?"

"The structure of it, for one thing," H.D. said. "This isn't a *town* like you and I would think of it. It's a bunch of little towns, all close together, each with a different set of rules and regulations. They call them 'parishes,' but really they're just little towns."

"That doesn't make a lick of sense," Fargo said. "Why don't they have a city council or something?"

"They do," he replied. "But as a rule, they're ignored or laughed at. The real power here is in who runs the parishes that produce the most money."

"Like Storyville," Fargo said.

"Exactly. There's Winn Parish and Catahoula Parish, which are really run by State Senators Parker and Beares. Storyville is part of both, and it's where the most money gets made. So the fighting has been fierce."

"Have you had any trouble?" Fargo asked.

H.D. chuckled and poured another set of shots. "No," he said. "And I don't intend to. I get paid by the city, have full retirement benefits, and do my best to keep peace in the streets. Which means that Anderson, Parker, and Beares have taken their battles to the alleys, the swamps, and the backrooms of the whorehouses. It suits me just fine to let them fight it out amongst themselves."

Fargo's eyes narrowed. This wasn't like the H.D. he'd known at all. "I thought you believed in the law," he said quietly.

"Fargo, I do," H.D. said. "But I'm not a young man anymore, and there's only one of me and three of them, plus more hired guns than you've ever seen. When they aren't shooting each other, they're knifing each other. And when they aren't doing that, they use their hands to choke, steal, or beat the hell out of anyone they can." He drank his shot and then added, "And now you're here."

"Just here for work," Fargo said. "Parker hired me up in St. Louis."

"To do what?" H.D. asked. "You've never been on the wrong side of the law before."

"And I'm not now," he said. "I guess they've decided to settle all of this with a poker game."

"A poker game?" H.D. asked. "Seriously?"

"That's what Parker said, and Anderson confirmed it."

"I'll be damned," H.D. said. "Things might settle down, then. What's your job in all this?"

"I'm supposed to keep the game fair," he said. He sipped his own shot, savoring the charcoal flavor on his tongue. "So I'm told."

"Fair, huh?" his old friend said. "You do know that all of them will cheat like there's no tomorrow."

"I suspected as much," Fargo said. "But then it will be fair."

"What do you mean?"

"If one man cheats, it's not fair," Fargo replied. "He's taking advantage of the others. But if *all* of them cheat, then it is fair. No one is playing by a different set of rules than anyone else."

H.D. laughed so hard he went into a coughing fit, and finished by mumbling, "Goddamn humidity," under his breath. He looked up, wiped his mouth, and said, "Don't stay down here too long. It's like breathing a swamp."

"I don't plan to," Fargo said. "Just long enough to do what I was hired to do, collect my pay, and move on."

"So where's this poker game being held?" H.D.

asked. "That way, maybe I can keep an eye on things outside at least."

"The Blue Emporium," Fargo said. "Hattie Hamilton's place."

H.D. hissed like a scalded cat. "Damn. That maybe changes everything."

"What do you mean?"

"She plays at belonging to Parker, but Hattie Hamilton belongs to nobody," H.D. said. "She's as cold-blooded a woman as I've ever met."

"She seemed decent enough to me," Fargo said. "She met Parker and me when we got here, down at the docks."

"That's Hattie, all right," he said. "She likes to play the lady, but she's more snake than woman."

"Come on, H.D.," Fargo said. "She's just a woman—and a whore to boot."

"Fargo, you listen and you listen close," H.D. said, his voice dropping to a whisper. "Hattie Hamilton has killed at least two people that I know of, though I could never prove it. And those girls of hers are barely more than slaves. She's got more money than Parker or Beares, and if they're holding this so-called game at her place, you better have sharp eyes, because something about her is . . . wrong, broken on the inside."

"Do you think she's dangerous?" Fargo asked. "Honestly?"

"Like a hungry alligator," H.D. said. "And she's damn near untouchable. Half the men in the state senate have either slept with her or been in her place. She knows lots of pillow secrets, and even when she's suspected of something, every deputy in this town will look the other way."

Fargo whistled, thinking that maybe he'd underestimated the players in the game. "I can't say as I'm much impressed with this place," he said. "Why do you stay?"

"Safer than being out west," he said. "Out there, in the open, there's nowhere to hide. Once a bad man moves into an area, you've either got to kill him, hang him, or arrest him—and if you're outnumbered, the odds are against it. Here, all I have to do is keep the streets quiet and go about my business. It's not justice, but I've learned that at least here, I've got places to hole up in."

"Didn't imagine you being much of a runner," Fargo said. "You stood and fought right next to me back in Kansas."

"This *isn't* Kansas, Fargo," H.D. snapped. "It's not like anywhere I've ever been or heard of. New Orleans sprang up out of a swamp, and in its rotten heart, it's still a swamp. If I weren't married, why I'd—"

"Married!" Fargo interrupted. "Since when?"

"I met her about two months after I got here," H.D. said. "Beautiful Creole girl. She won't leave because her family is here. Otherwise, retirement be damned, I'd have moved on."

"I'd like to meet her," Fargo said. "No wonder you're keeping your head down."

H.D.'s face reddened. "It's . . . it's worse than that, Fargo." He skipped the glass and knocked back another swallow of the sour mash. "She . . . she worked there. At the Blue Emporium. She was a whore."

"What?"

H.D. shook his head. "I ain't supposed to talk about it," he said. "But the truth is that Hattie Hamilton's had me by the short hairs since I got here. And if I do anything that messes with her, I'll be out of a job, probably dead, and my wife . . . she . . . she'd have to go back to work for Hattie."

"Damn," Fargo whispered. "You've landed in a world of trouble, haven't you?"

His old friend nodded, then said, "And now you're in it, too, Fargo. Once you've messed around in Storyville business, it's like a bear trap. You don't get free. Not ever."

"I'm my own man," Fargo said quietly. "I always have been."

"Not here," H.D. said. "No one here is free."

Looking into H.D.'s eyes, Fargo could see that his old friend believed what he was saying. Every word of it. Struck by the depths of despair, the lies and deceit all around him, Fargo finished his glass of whiskey and set it on the desk with a soft thump. "I guess I'll get over to the hotel," he said. "Maybe grab some dinner. Then I've got to find Beares. I want to talk to him before the game."

"Don't worry about it," H.D. said. "He'll find you." He poured himself another snort from the bottle, and Fargo saw that his friend's hands were steady, but his eyes were haunted. "He'll find you and then you'll have talked to them all and you'll know what I've told you is the truth. This place isn't a city, Fargo. It's an alligator pit, and each and every one of them is hungry."

"Damn," Fargo said again. He could never have imagined John H. D. Timmons this broken down inside, this scared of anyone. "What have I gotten myself into here?"

"A real bad place, Fargo. A *real* bad place."

6

Fargo took the Ovaro to the livery, mentioning Fleur to the owner, who got flustered and turned a shade of red Fargo hadn't seen since the last time he'd eaten beets. Still, the man ran a decent enough stable, and Fargo felt comfortable leaving his horse and tack there with only minimal questioning.

The man assured him that someone was on duty at all times. "Day or night, sir," he said. "Ain't no one messes with my place. I pay my dues."

"And you'll see to it that he gets his oats?" Fargo asked, hanging his saddle on a rack next to the stall they'd put the Ovaro in.

"Yes, sir," the man said, nodding his head like it was on a string. "Once a day, plus fresh hay and water. I'll watch after him."

"Good enough," Fargo said. He paid the man for a week's worth, even though he fully intended to be headed back west before then.

"That's more than you owe, Mr. Fargo," the livery man said.

"I know," Fargo replied. "I should be back for him within a few days. If I'm happy with his care when I get back, you can keep the rest as a tip."

Voice quavering, the man said, "And if you're not?"

Fargo's blue eyes stared hard at the man; then he said, "Then I'll take my money back—and not in a nice way." He'd already come to the conclusion that only force, threats of force, and excessive money bought much of anything in this place—three types of currency that he preferred not to use unless necessary.

"You'll be happy, Mr. Fargo," the man said, nodding his head again. "Happy as a gator with chicken bones."

Fargo shook his head, then grabbed up the rest of his gear and headed to the hotel, wondering about some of the strange sayings people had in this city. As much as he'd traveled, combing back and forth across the frontier, most of the people he'd run into talked pretty much as he did. The city of New Orleans was a strange place, almost a world of its own, and he'd be glad to leave it behind him.

He felt even more besieged by the city as he walked its streets now. Maybe it was the convergence of all the historical troubles that had taken place here. The French displacing the Indians, the French ceding control to Spain in a secret and unpopular treaty provision—and little more than a decade later French and German settlers forcing the Spanish governor to flee. And during all this, enormous epidemics of malaria, smallpox, and yellow fever, to name just a few of the terrible medical mishaps that thinned the population again and again.

Add to this the strange beliefs and cults that entangled so much of daily life in the city. The Cajuns with their swamp tales and myths, and the constant evidence of voodoo, that fevered belief system that merged Roman Catholicism with Haitian black magic. Many of the stores advertised that they sold trinkets of various kinds to combat spells and curses. The shopkeepers would smile ironically about them but deep down you had the sense that on some level at least they believed in these things.

Say what you wanted about bloody trail towns with all their shoot-outs and boot hills. But however troubled they were, they didn't dally with zombies and boiling pots of chicken parts meant to bring death to some unsuspecting person halfway across town.

Fargo had to smile at the thought of all this. He'd always heard about hell. But he'd never believed that he'd actually be able to walk its streets, not in this life, anyway.

But that was where he was, all right. New Orleans was hell on earth.

The room Fargo rented at the Bayou wasn't anything to write home about: a single bed, a cobbled-together wooden dresser with two long drawers topped by a scratched-up mirror, and a pitcher and basin that had once been white, but were now a sort of sooty grayish-brown color. Still, the sheets were clean and it had something else to recommend it: a door that actually locked.

Not that it would stop anyone serious about breaking in—the wood of the door was thin and the frame slightly warped—but it might deter the casual burglar and at least give him some few seconds of warning for the more serious.

Fargo considered his earlier meetings of the day, and particularly what his friend H.D. had told him. If what he'd said was true, there was no need to go looking for Senator Richard Beares—the man would find him.

The hotel itself didn't have a restaurant, but there was a diner right next door that looked somewhat promising. Maybe a decent meal would quell the feeling in his stomach that he'd made a deal with the devil, gone straight down to hell and ponied up the money to get the gates open so he could dance with the dead. It was an uncomfortable sensation and not one he wished to become overly familiar with.

"Sometimes," Fargo said to himself, "a man will up and do the damndest things for money." He stowed his saddlebags and clothing in the dresser drawers, taking the time to change into a clean blue shirt and freshly laundered denims. The riverboat offered many conveniences, including a beautiful waitress who had not only been a pleasure in bed, but had kindly done his laundry for him, too. He slipped on a tanned leather vest and buckled on his gun belt, double-checking the Colt's loads to make sure that the weapon was in good operating condition.

He'd seen too many men die for skipping simple firearms maintenance, and it was one thing he never failed to do: check his weapon every time he strapped it on. Plucking his hat off the bedpost, Fargo gave himself a quick once-over in the mirror and decided that while he could use a fresh shave, he was presentable enough for dinner, anyway.

He stepped out of his room, locking the door behind him. There was little in it of real value, and he had most of his funds in his belt, with some ready cash in a battered wallet he carried on the inside of his vest. His boots rapped on the hollow stairs as he went down, and he nodded at the man behind the small counter as he stepped out into the last light of the evening.

The sidewalks were crowded with people coming and going, and nearby, he could hear the singing of a Chinese man, punctuated by the *slap-snap* of clothing as he hung it on the line. At least that was the same, Fargo thought. Seemed like the last few years, every town he'd passed through had at least one Chinaman willing to give your clothes a decent washing, snap them in the air, and hang them on the line to dry—though as humid as the air was here, Fargo wondered if anything was ever really dry in this part of the world.

He made his way down the crowded sidewalk toward the sign that read BUTTERFIELD DINER, and below that: GOOD EATS. He stepped inside and found that the place was pretty busy, but there was still room enough at the counter for a man to sit down. He picked out a spot and looked for a place to set his hat, eventually settling for hooking it on his knee.

"Evening, mister," the man behind the counter said. He was Cajun, but didn't have a trace of the accent. "Special tonight is our own Butterfield Gumbo—it's a mite spicy so you'll want a beer with that. Only two bits."

"What's in it?" Fargo asked.

"The gumbo or the beer, sir?" the man said, laughing at his own joke before adding, "Fresh crawfish, caught just this very morning, Cajun sausage, some swamp onions, and other vittles. It's like a stew, but as I said, just a mite spicy."

It sounded interesting, and since he'd never had it, Fargo said, "Why not? I've had Mexican food that would melt stone."

"Excellent choice, mister," the man said, jotting his order on a pad. "I'll get it for you and be right back."

Fargo scanned the crowded room and the counter and noted that most of the people were dressed as town folk—suits and dresses, instead of denims and work shirts. Bowler hats were common, but only a few cowboy hats. Everything seemed peaceable enough, so he turned his attention back to the man behind the counter, who was headed his way with a large mug of beer in one hand and a steaming bowl in the other.

"Smells good," Fargo said as he set the bowl down in front of him, reaching under the counter and then placing a paper napkin and a spoon next to the bowl.

But when the man was distracted momentarily, Fargo went back to scanning the guests. One other thing Fargo didn't like much about this city was the way it treated the so-called "Free People of Color." This meant the Creoles and the slaves. Most of them worked on the docks for mercilessly long hours and very little pay. It was people such as these filling the restaurant that profited more than they should have from the work of the poor.

The slaves were leased out by their masters for dock work. They were allowed to keep a pittance of what they earned. Their masters promised the slaves that if they saved their money they would be allowed to buy their freedom someday.

All this had been going on since the first steamship docked in New Orleans early in the century.

But the Haitians who came here after the slave revolt in their native land, the Creoles, and the American slaves all fooled those who would hold them back. By 1850 they'd started buying up properties and starting small businesses. And with more and more slaves freed, the whole community of Free People of Color was beginning to have at least a small say in how the city treated them.

"You'll love it," the man said, getting back to Fargo and grinning. He turned around and pulled a small loaf of cornbread with butter in a tiny dish off the back counter. "You'll want this, too," he said. "If it's too hot for you, the bread will help cool things off a bit."

Fargo chuckled. "Like I said, I've eaten Mexican food." He picked up the spoon and stirred the dark-brown concoction. It smelled a little spicy, and he could see the ground-up sausage and the crawfish tails and vegetables floating in the gravy. "I'm sure I'll be fine."

"You might want to—"

He dove in, taking a large spoonful and putting it in his mouth.

The first sensation was the flavor—dark and rich, like a good stew—and the curious combination of the crawfish and the sausage. For a moment, Fargo thought maybe he'd found the only thing in New Orleans worth telling anyone about. Then the second sensation hit him: a slight tingle on his tongue and lips, a vague heat on the sides of his mouth that suddenly exploded into pure, burning agony.

He glanced at the man behind the counter who was watching him expectantly. Fargo felt his face redden and his eyes begin to water.

"I tried to warn you, sir," the man said, trying to contain his smile. "It *is* a mite spicy."

Fargo wanted to speak, but all that came out was a weak-sounding cough. This was nothing like Mexican food. This was like swallowing a campfire ember that sat in your mouth and stayed there, burning and burning, searing away your own spit.

"The bread, sir," the man said, gesturing to the bowl. "It will help."

Fargo opted for the beer instead, whipping the glass off the bar and taking several large swallows.

Distantly, he heard the man try to say something, but all he could think about was getting the fire out of his mouth. The problem, he soon discovered, was that the beer only washed the flames farther down his throat.

"Oh, my God," he gasped out. Tears streamed down his face.

The man held up the bread, and Fargo snatched it from his hand, slathered it with butter—didn't he hear somewhere that butter helped burns?—and shoved a big piece in his mouth. Almost immediately, the bread did its work, and the pain began to ease.

After a few seconds, the sensation calmed down to an almost tolerable heat and the flavor of the gumbo emerged again—dark, rich, and delicious. "Whew," Fargo managed. "You do know what the word 'mite' means, don't you?"

"Yes, sir," the man said, now grinning openly. " 'Just a little.' You should try our really spicy version. Last week, it nearly killed a man."

"How . . ." Fargo stopped, ate another piece of bread, and took a swallow of beer. "How do you manage to eat that stuff, let alone sell it?"

"I tried to tell you, sir," the man said, his head bowing down. "It's better if you dip the bread in it. That's what it's for."

"Then why'd you give me a spoon?" Fargo demanded.

The man sighed. "If I tried to tell you it was too hot, you wouldn't have believed me, sir!"

Fargo thought about it a minute, then began to chuckle ruefully. "I suppose you're right." The flavor was nice, so he said, "Dip the bread into it?"

The man nodded. "Go ahead," he said. "It's not half as bad the second time."

Fargo tried it, dipping the cornbread into the gumbo, and found it to be much more tolerable. In fact, it was like nothing he'd ever had and he found himself setting to with a vengeance. "How do you get it so spicy?" he asked, between bites.

"Family secret," the man said. "But part of it is the pepper oil."

"Pepper oil?" he asked. "What's pepper oil?"

"If you squeeze certain types of peppers, you get a tiny amount of liquid that is very hot. By itself, it can cause blisters on the skin. So we dilute it, of course, but it still adds a lot of heat to the gumbo. But it's good, yes?"

Fargo had to admit it *was* delicious, despite the fact that even with the bread and the beer, he knew he'd be feeling the heat of the meal two hours later. "Yes," he said. "It is good. Just not something you'd want to dive into without instruction."

"No, sir," the man said. His eyes widened a bit, and he was about to say something else, when Fargo felt a heavy hand come down on his shoulder.

"You Skye Fargo?" a deep voice asked from behind him.

Fargo didn't turn around, but said, "Who wants to know?"

The hand squeezed his shoulder, and the voice said, "*I'm* asking you, and if you don't want a broken collarbone to go with your dinner, you'll answer."

So fast that the man behind the counter gasped aloud, Fargo spun on his stool, catching the man's hand in his own, reversing it and yanking the fingers down. Several broke with an audible *crack*ing sound and the man let out a muffled whimper. It was muffled because as he'd gone down, Fargo had shoved his knee into the man's face, breaking several teeth.

He saw that there was a second man behind him, reaching for his gun.

"I wouldn't," Fargo warned. He twisted slightly and shoved the man with the broken hand to the ground, pulling his Colt with blazing speed. He had it pointed at the other man before his pistol could clear leather.

"Drop it," Fargo snapped. "Back into the holster, nice and easy."

The man did as he was told, then raised his hands. His partner on the ground managed to get to his feet, but his lips and nose were bloody ruins and three of the fingers on his right hand were twisted and broken.

"Let me guess," Fargo said, keeping his gun pointed at them. "You were sent to bring me to Senator Beares."

"That's right," the broken-fingered man said. "He wants to see you."

"I take it he's not used to being refused," Fargo said.

"You can come with us now," the other man said, "or we'll leave and come back with a dozen guns to take you the hard way."

"Hey, Ratty," the man behind the counter said. "Looks like the only folks getting the hard way so far is you and Puncher."

"Shut up," Ratty said. "You don't want to cross us, Fargo. Why not make it easy and come along and see what the Senator has to say?"

Fargo cocked his gun and their eyes went wide. "Or I could just kill you both," he said evenly, "finish my dinner, and go on about my business." He glanced around the room. "I imagine most everyone in here will say it was self-defense."

"He just wants to talk to you, mister," Puncher said, holding his hand. "Just talk."

"Then why try to force me at all?" Fargo said.

"We heard you was a tough guy, is all," Ratty replied. "Figured we'd have to use force."

"You couldn't force me to blink," he replied. He glanced at a nearby table, then gestured with the Colt. "Take a seat," he said.

"What?" Puncher said. "Why?"

"Because I said so," Fargo said, turning the Colt back in his direction. The size of the bore must have made an impression because both Ratty and Puncher moved to sit down.

Once they were seated, Fargo sat back down on his own chair. "Now, sit there, be quiet, and don't cause trouble," he said. "When I'm finished with my meal, we'll go find your boss."

"He said to bring you *now*," Ratty whined. "He don't like waiting on no one."

"Then he should've sent me a note," Fargo said. "You've got a choice, Ratty. Sit there, shut up, and let me eat in peace, or I'll send you back to Senator Beares so full of holes, he'll change your name to Cheese."

Ratty looked like he was going to say something more, but discretion got the better of him and he snapped his mouth shut.

"Good," Fargo said. He turned back to the gumbo. "You boys hungry?" he asked, not looking their way. "The gumbo here is a mite spicy, but it's delicious."

"He's not tough," Puncher mumbled under his breath. "He's crazy. That gumbo could melt lead."

Fargo ignored him and finished his meal, keeping one hand close to the Colt at all times. When he'd finished, he put a dollar on the bar. "There you go, mister," he said. "I don't reckon I'll ever forget that meal."

"It's only two bits, Mr. Fargo," the man said. "Let me get you your change."

Fargo shook his head. "No, the rest is a tip. What's on the menu for tomorrow?"

The man behind the counter grinned. "Blackened alligator steaks," he said. "They're a mite—"

"Spicy," Fargo finished for him. "I'll look forward to it."

He put his hat on and gestured to Ratty and Puncher. "Let's go see your boss," he said. They stood and he followed them out into the New Orleans night.

Most of the towns Fargo had ever been in, the small cattle towns that dotted the western landscape, went pretty quiet after sundown. Even the saloons weren't all that noisy unless a bunch of cowpunchers got paid and came in to raise a little hell. But for the most part, after dark, the towns of the West were quiet places. The folks who lived there worked too hard during the day to kick up much of a fuss at night.

But New Orleans was a different place after dark. An entirely new population walked the streets. Heavy-browed men looking for prostitutes, thieves skulking in alleyways looking for tourists who didn't know the danger that surrounded them, whores calling out from balcony windows—some of them showing more skin than clothing—and then there were the children. All ages and skin colors raced through the streets, but all of them were dirt poor. They were out scavenging, looking for the scraps of the day, trying to find enough food to eat.

Following Ratty and Puncher through the maze of streets, Fargo kept his eyes and senses alert for trouble. There was no telling when they'd run across either more of Senator Beares' men or a contingent of men belonging to Anderson or Parker. Both men walked in front of him, their shoulders tense, their heads swiveling on their necks as though if they tried hard enough, they could see right through the shadows around them to whatever danger might be approaching.

After several blocks, they turned and began to relax, eventually leading him to a house with a heavy iron gate in front of it. "This is it," Ratty said. "Go on through the gate and up to the door. Just knock and ol' Charles will let you in to see the senator."

"No," Fargo said. "You open the gate, Ratty. I think the two of you will make fine escorts all the way to the senator."

"Ain't nothing going to happen to you, Fargo," Puncher said. "He just wants to talk is all."

"Then he wouldn't have sent heavy-handed thugs like you," Fargo snapped. "Now get moving."

Ratty turned the handle and opened the gate, which squealed on its hinges. Tiny leaves from the ivy growing along the gate fell to the ground. "Go on in, boys," Fargo said. "I'll be right behind you."

"Aw, shit," Puncher said. "I sure hope they don't shoot us by accident."

"That would be a shame," he said. "I'd feel awful."

"Mister, you wouldn't give a rat's ass if we both died."

"Not true," Fargo quipped. "I'm willing to give them two asses—a Puncher's and a Ratty's. Now get inside and be quick about it."

They moved forward and Fargo's eyes scanned the shadowy darkness.

Beares' men were there—he could feel them—and a telltale flicker of movement on the roof caught his eye. Two men were stationed up there, holding rifles.

They were nearly at the front door, when Fargo barked, "Stop there!"

Both men stopped dead in their tracks.

"Senator," Fargo shouted, his voice echoing strangely off the stone of the house. "Be a shame if we couldn't talk because all your men were dead. Call them off or I'll cut down Ratty and Puncher, and then those two men you've got on the roof."

A voice floated into the courtyard from an open window.

"There's no need for violence yet, Mr. Fargo," it said. "Stand down, boys. This one can come in."

The front door opened and an elderly butler stood in the doorway. "Please, Mr. Fargo," he said, his ancient voice cracking. "The senator will see you now."

"Keep moving, Ratty, Puncher," he said. "I'd hate to have you slip away and leave me all by my lonesome."

"Aww, shit," Ratty mumbled. "Could this night get any worse?"

"You could get dead," Fargo said. "Now get inside."

They stepped through the door and Fargo followed them, wondering as he did so, if getting back out again was going to present the same set of problems, only with his back to Beares' men, instead of his front.

It was an unpleasant thought, and Fargo knew that if he was going to get out of here alive, he'd have to play the game that was about to unfold very carefully.

7

From the entryway, Fargo saw that to the left was some sort of parlor or living room, furnished with heavy, padded couches and chairs, formal lamps, and an air of stuffiness to it that reminded him of people with too much money and not enough hard work to do. In his experience, a little hard labor went a long way toward teaching a man the value of a dollar.

The butler Charles moved with a kind of aging grace, his movements smooth despite the burden of his years. Fargo, with Ratty and Puncher in front of him, followed behind as Charles led them into another room to the right.

Fargo had not entered a mere house. He had entered an entirely different world from the one he was used to. This was antebellum New Orleans, the world of money and high society, of vast parties and privilege, of carriages trimmed in real gold, of opera companies imported from Italy and France, of horse races where tens of thousands of dollars were spent on single events. French was often spoken within these walls and very real duels were sometimes fought at drunken outdoor parties on the land in back of these mighty mansions.

Fargo wondered where the butler had been imported from. He certainly looked like the real thing. Formal but not unpleasant, businesslike but approachable.

This room was more to Fargo's liking: dark wood paneling, leather chairs with brass rivets, a fireplace on one wall, a bar on another, and at one end a heavy, wooden desk made of polished mahogany. Over the fireplace there was a mounted lion's head. Senator Beares sat in one of the chairs, sipping on a drink.

"Ahh, thank you, Charles," he said. His voice was even, but beneath it, Fargo heard the tones of a man who was used to being in command and wasn't afraid of much of anything. "Mr. Fargo," he said, "please, consider yourself my guest. There's no need for your weapon. You have my word—no harm will come to you here, at least no harm of my making."

"That's why you sent Ratty and Puncher to bring me here? Because you don't intend me any harm?"

"Ratty and Puncher tend to be a little . . . overenthusiastic at times," Beares said. He turned his gaze to the men. "I believe I instructed you to be gentle with Mr. Fargo. Did you fail me in this?"

"Hell, no!" Puncher said. "I just grabbed him a little is all, on the shoulder like, to show him we were serious." He held out his mangled hand to demonstrate, then added, "Look what the sonofabitch did to me!"

Beares rose from his seat, taking a closer look at his employee, then turning back to the bar. "That does appear painful, Puncher," he said. "You also appear to be missing at least one tooth and your nose isn't a pretty sight either." He shook his head. "I should've sent Charles. He, at least, would have been wise enough not to risk laying a hand on Mr. Fargo."

He made a shooing gesture. "Ratty, Puncher, you are dismissed," he said. "Ratty, you will take Puncher to the doctor and have him seen to. Puncher, once you are done there, you will report back here and Charles will give you your pay. Then you are to leave New Orleans. If you return here, I will have you dealt with the way I do anyone who disobeys my orders."

"Aww, but Senator—"

"Shut *up*, Puncher," Ratty interjected. "You know what will happen. Just do as the man says."

"Fine," Puncher snapped, spinning on his heels. "I don't need no doctor. Just pay me and I'll go."

"Very well," Beares said. He picked up a small bell on the bar and rang it. In moments, Charles appeared at the doorway.

"You rang, sir?" he asked. Fargo noted that his voice held the very slightest of accents, as though it had been worn away by years of disuse.

"Yes, Charles," Beares said. "Please pay Puncher for two weeks' work, and see to it that he takes his horse and gear out of the stable. He is leaving my employ."

"This is all *your* fault, Fargo," Puncher said. "This ain't over. Not by a long shot."

Fargo eyed the man and nodded. "Maybe we should settle it right now, Puncher, though I reckon you're more the type to sneak up on a man from behind than you are to face him straight on."

"You calling me a coward?" Puncher snarled.

"No," Fargo said. "You *are* a coward. I'm not making suggestions."

"That's it!" Puncher snapped, his hand flashing toward his gun.

Fargo reached for his Colt, but before he could clear leather another shot rang out. He looked to see that Charles was holding a small pistol in his hands. Puncher blinked—once, twice, like he was thinking about something real hard—then fell dead at Fargo's feet.

"You dumbass, Puncher," Ratty said. "Why'd you have to go and do that?"

Fargo made eye contact with Charles, who simply nodded. The man was lightning fast, and suddenly Fargo realized why he was so close to Beares. He was his bodyguard and some kind of a shootist to boot.

"A clear case of defense," Beares said. "Well done, Charles."

Fargo stepped over the prone body of Puncher and stopped in front of the butler. "You're more than what you seem," he said quietly, pitching his voice low. "Who are you?"

"Aren't we all, Mr. Fargo?" Charles replied. "The senator said you would not be harmed while you were here; I was simply ensuring that his word remained unbroken."

"Ratty, carry Puncher here outside, then clean up the mess," Beares said. "Mr. Fargo, can I pour you a whiskey?"

Nodding coolly to the so-called butler, Fargo turned his attention back to the man who'd brought him here. "All right," he said, realizing that Charles—whoever he really was—wasn't going to answer his question. "Make mine a double."

Fargo and Beares sat quietly, sipping their drinks and not saying much of anything, while Ratty and Charles removed Puncher's dead body and cleaned up the mess. Once they were alone, Beares nodded in satisfaction.

"Nothing is ever easy, is it, Mr. Fargo?" he asked. "I simply wanted to have a few words with the man who's the talk of Storyville tonight, and instead, things got . . . complicated."

"They have a way of doing that," Fargo replied. "What do you want with me, Senator?"

"I hear interesting things about you, Mr. Fargo. You show up, apparently working for Parker, then ride off for a while, come back, break up a fight in which some of my men were teaching that Anderson boy a thing or two about manners, meet with that upstanding beacon of justice Timmons, and finally wind up here—beating up another one of my men before my own butler had to shoot him dead." Beares sighed heavily. "You've had a long day, Fargo."

"True enough," he admitted. "But you're forgetting something, Senator."

"What's that?"

"I was having my dinner and not bothering you or anyone else, when your men found me and 'asked' me to come along. My original plan had been to try to see you tomorrow."

Beares laughed. "You shoot straight, don't you, Fargo? I like that in a man, and it's how I prefer to behave myself."

"Is that right?"

"It is. It is," Beares said. He pointed to the lion's head above the fireplace. "I killed that creature myself, Fargo. On safari in Africa. And do you know what I learned there?"

"What's that?"

"That despite all our so-called civilized advances, the law of the jungle still applies. The strong survive. The weak die off or are killed. Man is superior to animals, Fargo, but only because of intellect. And despite your appearance, you seem to me to be a man of intellect."

"How's that?" Fargo asked.

"You may not boast a superior education, but you think things through. You like to know about everything going on around you—the people, the land, everything—so that you can judge for yourself what is of value and what is not." He took a sip of his bourbon. "You are your own man, even if you are working for that conniving bastard, Parker."

"Is everyone here crooked?" Fargo asked bluntly. "So far, not a single person I've met has a decent thing to say about the other, and I reckon you're about the same in that regard. As you said, Senator, I've had a long day. Can we skip the part about how Parker and Anderson are thieves and bad men and all you want to do is help Storyville? Can we just get to what you want from me?"

Beares laughed long and loud. "As I said, you shoot straight." He stood and poured himself another drink. "All right, Fargo, I'll do the same. There are three of us vying for control of Storyville—the parishes of Winn and Catahoula, to be precise. We all think we're entitled, and none of us is really better than the robber barons of England or the pirates that ply the Caribbean. I know you're working for Parker, and I wanted to see what I could do about that."

"Not much," Fargo said. "I've taken the man's money and given him my word."

"To do what, precisely?" Beares asked.

"To keep the game fair," Fargo said. "He suspects that one or more of the players may cheat, and he wants me to keep an eye on it, catch the person if I can."

Beares brought the bottle from the bar and offered Fargo a refill, but he shook his head. "I've had enough, thanks."

"And will you do it, then?" Beares asked. "Keep the game fair?"

"As much as I can," Fargo replied. "The game will be fair so long as everyone plays by the same rules."

"And since when," a familiar voice said from the doorway, "is a lady required to play by the rules?"

Fargo looked up, more than a little surprised to see Hattie Hamilton framed in the doorway.

Beares rose to his feet, and Fargo followed suit. "Ah, good evening, my dear," he said. "Can I pour you a drink?"

"Do you even have to ask?" Hattie said, striding into the room. "I've been dealing with David all day."

"Understood," Beares said, moving to the bar and pouring her a stiff jolt. "This should help settle your nerves." He handed her the glass and she took a long swallow, then sighed in pleasure. "Better?" he asked.

She nodded. "It's a start," she said, then turned to Fargo. "You've had a busy day yourself, Mr. Fargo," she said. "The parish talk is all about you—fighting in the streets, running into old friends, even giving my young Fleur a ride back from her little outing to the countryside."

Fargo winced inwardly, knowing that the young lady had not wanted to be seen. For a town with so many secrets, it seemed like very little went on that the people in power didn't know about. "I've been busy," he admitted. "Now I'm curious."

"And what are you curious about, Mr. Fargo?" Hattie asked, settling herself on the long leather couch and leaning back in a provocative pose. Once again, her eyes screamed seduction, but he reminded himself of H.D.'s warning.

"Based on what I saw down at the docks, you and Senator Parker are an item," Fargo said. "I'd go so far as to say he seemed very possessive of you. And now you're here—with a man he would say was an enemy."

Hattie laughed, and the sound reminded Fargo of some wind chimes he'd once heard—light and melodic—and warning of the coming storm as the winds rose. "Well, Mr. Fargo, a lady does need more than one patron if she's going to make her way in the world." She batted her long eyelashes at him, then said, "Isn't that right, dear?"

"Quite right, Hattie," Beares said. He seated himself next to her and put a hand on her thigh. "But I think that Mr. Fargo is a smart enough man to realize that there's quite a bit more going on here than meets the eye."

"He looks like a dirty cowboy to me," she said. "But with a bath and some proper clothing, I suspect he'd clean up rather well."

"I'm not a city man," Fargo said. "I wear what's functional out on the trail and not much else."

"After this week, you'll be a wealthy man, Mr. Fargo," Hattie said. "I imagine that you'll soon get used to the things money can buy: comfortable clothing, good whiskey, beautiful women."

Trying to turn the tables on her a bit, Fargo grinned lecherously. "The beautiful women part I've got licked."

She smiled in return. "I bet you do. I wonder . . ."

"That's quite enough of that, Hattie," Beares interjected. "She's almost insatiable, Fargo. You'll have to excuse her more predatory appetites." He growled at her almost playfully. "We have business to discuss with Mr. Fargo, my dear. We should try to keep to the matter at hand."

"Of course, Beary," she said. "Whatever you wish."

She made the words sound like a promise of other things—things best done in a darkened bedroom—and Beares laughed. "I'll hold you to that," he said.

"What business?" Fargo asked. "I'd like to get back to my hotel and get some sleep."

"Simple," Beares said. "We want you to work for us, Mr. Fargo. The poker game is far too important to allow Senator Parker *or* that petty criminal Anderson to win. The future of New Orleans is at stake."

"I've already agreed to work for Senator Parker," Fargo said evenly. "I told you that."

"We're well aware of your arrangement with Senator Parker," Beares said. "We simply ask that you work for us, too."

"How so?" Fargo asked. "I've already said I'll keep the game fair."

"Oh, no," Hattie said. "This has nothing to do with keeping the game fair. We have something else entirely in mind."

Fargo suspected as much. They wanted him to double-cross Parker so they could win somehow. "I'm not the kind of man who believes in going back on his word."

"We expect nothing of the sort," Beares said. "Your friend H.D. made your reputation in this town since long before your arrival: a man of justice and all that. We want you to do nothing that will violate your word to Senator Parker."

"Then what do you want?" Fargo asked again, his patience wearing thin. "Just spit it out."

"We want to hire you to protect us," Hattie said, leaning forward. "Between Anderson and . . . and David . . . we are constantly under threat of attack. How can the game be fair if my lovely Beary is killed before it even happens?"

"Seems like you've got plenty of men to do that," Fargo said. "And your 'butler' Charles—whoever he really is—is a pretty fair hand with a gun himself."

"Ahh, it's not for me," Beares said. "Despite Hattie's good intentions, I'm perfectly safe. My concern is for her. Should Parker find out about us . . . or if things go badly for him at the game . . . I fear he may do something rash where Hattie is concerned." He looked at Fargo earnestly. "I simply want you to look out for her, Fargo. Even a man such as yourself might understand why she is my most prized trophy."

"She's something," Fargo admitted, trying to work his mind around the situation. Something wasn't right about all of this, but he wasn't sure what it was. "Again," he said, "why me? You've got plenty of help. Just assign one of them to do it."

"Parker knows most of my men by sight, Fargo," Beares explained. "Should he or one of his men try to harm Hattie, he would never suspect that I've employed you to keep her safe."

"Besides," Hattie added, "you wouldn't want to see me get hurt, would you, Mr. Fargo?"

"I don't hold with harming women in general," Fargo said, thinking again of H.D.'s words and wondering if Hattie was more snake than human. "And what will you pay me for this?" he asked, playing for time.

"We've considered that," Beares said, "and I believe we have just the compensation in mind that would interest you." He gestured, and said, "Go on, Hattie. Tell him."

"When you leave New Orleans, Mr. Fargo, you'll be wealthy," Hattie said. "Between what David is paying you, and a reasonable cash incentive from us, you'll be able to make your way comfortably anywhere in the world. But your true reward from us you've already seen." She paused dramatically, then whispered, "I'll let you take Fleur when you go."

"Mary?" Fargo asked.

"I suppose that's her real name," Hattie said. "She is quite beautiful, isn't she, Mr. Fargo?"

Damn woman, Fargo thought. *How could he refuse if it meant getting Mary out of the horrible situation she was in?*

"Ah," Beares said. "I believe we've caught Mr. Fargo's interest."

"Oh, Beary," she said. "There's not a man alive who doesn't think with his pecker most of the time. It's why my business is so successful."

"Well, Fargo, what do you think of our little proposition? You keep Hattie here safe, and when the game is over, I'll give you two thousand in cash, plus Hattie will give you the beautiful Fleur for your very own. With what Parker is paying you, that's quite a haul for little more than a night's work."

"She's not a slave," Fargo said. "Someone you can just give away or sell whenever you want."

Hattie laughed. "Oh, Mr. Fargo, you are indeed naive about the ways of our city. Fleur is a slave in all but name. When she came to work for me, she signed a contract. A lifetime contract, Mr. Fargo. She is mine to do with as I please—and if giving her to you is what pleases me, then so be it." She waved a hand covered with a lace glove. "She'll go along quietly, Fargo. And from what the girls tell me, she was quite taken with you."

Damn woman, Fargo thought again. She'd maneuvered him into a corner. Somehow, she had a hold on something that Mary valued—maybe a hold of some kind over all the girls at the Blue Emporium. But in order to find out what it was, he'd have to play along. At least for a while.

"And all I have to do is keep Miss Hamilton safe?" he asked.

"Indeed," Beares said. "Even Senator Parker, I think, could respect that."

Fargo nodded, thinking that there was so much going on in this town that was beneath the surface. Everyone's motives were hidden and he suspected that the person truly pulling the strings was Hattie Hamilton—but what he lacked was proof.

"All right," he said. "I'll do it. For *Mary* and five thousand."

"Outrageous!" Beares shouted. "You can't be serious!"

Fargo grinned at him. "Oh, I imagine your 'most prized trophy' is worth at least that, isn't she, Senator Beares?"

"Damn women," Beares muttered. "Fine. Five thousand."

Hattie squealed like a schoolgirl and threw her arms around Beares. "You're so sweet, Beary," she said. "Whatever would I do without you?"

"Yes, well, there is that, isn't there?" Beares asked. He moved to a picture on the wall, removed it, and opened a safe. He took out a wad of cash and counted quickly. "Here's half now," he said to Fargo, handing it to him. "You'll get Fleur and the rest *after* the game is over and you're ready to leave town."

"Fair enough," Fargo said. "There's just one more thing."

"What's that?" they asked, almost in unison.

"Her name is *Mary*, and she doesn't take another customer from now on."

"What?" Hattie said. "What difference does it make?"

"Those are my terms," Fargo said. He held out the money to Beares. "Take it or leave it."

"What's it matter, Hattie?" Beares asked.

"I was hoping to . . ." She sighed, then nodded. "Fine, Mr. Fargo. *Mary* won't take another customer—but she stays at the Blue Emporium until it's all over."

"Agreed," Fargo said, slipping the money into his vest. "I'll be leaving now," he added. "If we're done?"

Beares was looking at Hattie hungrily and he waved Fargo away. "Of course, Fargo, by all means. I'm glad we were able to reach an understanding."

Fargo nodded and headed for the exit, wincing as he heard Hattie mutter behind him. "Men! They think with their peckers and believe theirs should be the only plow in the field."

"Of course we do, darling," Beares replied. "Speaking of plowing . . ."

Fargo quickened his pace, hoping that he'd get back

to his hotel room without any other adventures. He'd had more than enough for one day and his head was spinning with all the secrets and lies he'd heard . . . and all the money in his pocket.

8

Fargo made his way back to the Bayou without incident, his mind working on all the things he'd learned during the day's events, while his eyes scanned the crowded streets, keeping alert for any sign of trouble. Given how rowdy many of the saloons seemed to be, he somewhat expected it, but other than having to step out of the way of a man headed for an alleyway to throw up, no one bothered him.

Worn out from his day, Fargo nodded briefly to the man behind the counter and trudged up the stairs to his room. What he wanted now was a good night's sleep. Perhaps in the morning, with a decent breakfast and some coffee in him, he'd be able to figure out what was really going on here—hopefully before the poker game got under way and the powder keg all these people were sitting on blew sky-high.

He started to insert his key in the lock, but the door creaked open when he leaned a hand against it. Instantly awake, Fargo pulled his Colt, shoving himself against the wall and listening for any sounds. The room was quiet and dark, so he spun back into the doorway and kicked it wide open, shoving his Colt before him.

A high-pitched gasp of surprise stopped him in his tracks. "Please! Don't shoot me!"

"Mary?" Fargo asked, trying to adjust his eyes to the darkness. "Is that you?"

"Yes," she said, her voice quavering. "It's . . . it's Mary."

"Hold on a minute," Fargo said. He fumbled a match out of his vest, struck it against his thumb and lit the oil lamp. Light warmed the room as he turned up the wick a little bit. He turned to the girl, who was curled up beneath the thin blankets on his bed. Her skin glowed softly in the dim light, a deep, rich brown that reminded him a little of light molasses.

"What are you doing here, Mary?"

"Miz Hamilton," the girl said. "She told me to come over here before she left the Blue Emporium. I didn't ask too many questions, but please, don't hit me none. I still have to work."

"Ah, hell," Fargo said. *Hattie Hamilton is one cocky lady.* "I'm not going to hit you, Mary. I don't treat women that way." Even in the dimly lit room, he could see she was shaking in fear.

"You promise?" she asked.

"I promise," Fargo said. He sat down at the foot of the bed—there was nowhere else to sit in the room.

"I'll . . . I'll go back now," she said. "Miz Hamilton said if I didn't please you, I was to go back and she'd send another girl." She started to climb from beneath the blankets and Fargo's heart sped up a bit.

"What!" he exclaimed. "No, wait. I like you fine, Mary. I just . . . I wasn't expecting you, is all." He patted the bed. "Stay . . . please."

She sank back down and seemed to relax a little. "Thank you—"

"Call me Fargo," he said. "Or Skye, if you like."

Mary considered this for a moment, then said, "Skye, then. It's a nice name."

"Thank you," Fargo said. He was tired and had absorbed too much information in a short time—he needed to think and to rest.

"Skye," Mary said, her voice almost a whisper. "I don't understand why Miz Hamilton . . . she ain't never sent me out like this. I don't understand."

Fargo chuckled. "I can't say as I completely do, either." He pulled off his boots and unbuckled his gun belt, leaning forward to hang it over the bedpost.

"Probably best if we get some sleep and try to figure it out tomorrow."

"Sleep?" Mary asked. "I thought . . . you don't think I'm pretty, Skye?"

He looked over the beautiful young woman lying in his bed and smiled. With her dark hair and skin, she looked like a ribbon of chocolate silk against the white of the bedcovers. "I think you're very pretty," he said. He got to his feet and undressed, enjoying the sound when she gasped quiet appreciation at his flat, rock-hard stomach muscles and lean form.

He was down to only his underdrawers when she got out of the bed and turned down the lamp until the room was little more than pockets of dark gold light and shadows. The window shade was drawn and the noise from the street below faded into the background as he felt more than saw her come closer, running her hands down his chest.

"You been hurt a lot," she said. "Lots of scars."

"I've got a few," he said. Her hands roamed over the terrain of his shoulders, her nails lightly scratching. "But compared to those who gave them to me, I came out okay."

Her hands found his biceps and she said, "You're strong."

She moved lower, her hands seeking his manhood. Even if she wasn't often given pleasure for herself, she certainly knew how to give it as she stroked him to full hardness, then took him in her warm mouth. Using her tongue, she worked the shaft, base to tip and back again, warm and wet. Her hands found his sac and gently worked on him. Fargo's hands found her hair and he groaned in pleasure.

Finally, when he couldn't take it anymore, he eased away, pulling her to her feet. Mary kept her silence, her eyes wide open. Keeping his own silence, Fargo removed the nightgown, lifting it over her head. Her breasts fell free, rounded and full, but not overly large, with rose-colored areolas and pert nipples. Stepping closer, Fargo lowered his head and took one in his mouth, using his opposite hand to caress and stroke the nipple of the other. He felt them harden.

Her thighs were smooth and muscular, leading down to shapely calves. He knew it was time to please her. Her legs splayed open, giving him full access to her treasures, and Fargo didn't hesitate to explore the offerings on display to the fullest extent possible. He used his hands, his fingers, and his tongue, touching her, tasting her, arousing her senses everywhere he touched until she writhed on the bed, moaning and begging. Her breath came in short, sharp pants and Fargo knew she was ready, right on the edge of orgasm.

He quickened his pace, moving himself atop her and sliding into her warm center in one smooth motion. She shrieked in pleasure, rocketing to her climax as her hips shuddered beneath him.

"Oh, my God, my God!" she screamed, shoving herself against him. "Eeee . . . Yes, Skye! Yes, oh God, yes!" she screamed as her orgasm hit.

Her body shook beneath him, her hard nipples jutting into the air and the sweat on her skin making it shine. Fargo let himself go when he felt her clench his manhood, the sweet, musky scent of her orgasm hitting his nostrils and filling the air.

In the dim light he saw her small, wondering smile and she curled into the protective curve of his arm, sated and giving off an almost visible glow. After they'd gathered their breath, Fargo gently lifted her up and beneath the blanket, then joined her as she drifted into sleep.

Tired in mind and body, Fargo let himself wind down until sleep came on quiet feet to take him, too. His last thought was one of some concern and he promised himself to think on it more:

If Hattie Hamilton had sent the girl here before *he'd met with Beares, was it possible that she was playing some kind of game of her own?*

But it turned out not to be his last thought, after all. Suddenly he was awake again. He lay there listening to Mary breathing. Snoring, really. The soft, sweet sounds a child makes while sleeping. He smiled, grateful for an image of innocence in a city that knew very little innocence of any kind.

He reached over and touched her hip beneath the sheet. He envied her ability to fall asleep. There were so many angles and lies to sort through in this place. You couldn't be sure of anybody. Sometimes you even doubted yourself, something Skye Fargo wasn't used to.

He forced himself to close his eyes. To drive all thoughts of conspiracy from his mind. He wouldn't be much good if he had to drag through the day, now would he? But when sleep came it was troubled sleep with dreams of shadowy doorways and cards dealt from the bottoms of decks and smiling faces that were not at all what they seemed.

As was his habit, Fargo awoke early and took a moment before opening his eyes, letting his other senses tell him about his surroundings. The streets of New Orleans were beginning the slow process of waking up—unlike frontier towns that often started even before sunrise, New Orleans was a city of night, and it woke like an ill-used prostitute, slow and cranky and stiff.

It suddenly hit him that Mary wasn't in the bed. He opened his eyes and saw that the room was empty. He sat up, wondering where she'd gone and had just decided to go find her when the door handle rattled and began to turn.

With lightning reflexes, Fargo snagged his Colt free from its holster on the end of the bed and spun back to the door just as it opened.

Mary let out a little gasp of surprise and almost dropped the tray laden with breakfast and coffee she held in her hands. "Oh!" she said.

Fargo eased the hammer back on the Colt and put it away. "Sorry," he said. "I didn't know where you'd gone."

She blushed a bit, her dark-skinned cheeks showing just a hint of rose. "I'm sorry . . . Skye. I thought you'd like some coffee and food."

Fargo nodded appreciatively. "You reckoned right," he said. "I worked up a fairly good appetite last night."

She giggled and stepped the rest of the way into the room, setting the tray on the dresser and pouring coffee for him. Handing him the cup, she looked briefly into his eyes and the knowledge of the previous night once more made her blush. "Here," she said. "I made it myself."

Fargo grinned and took the cup, enjoying the hot feel of it in his hands. He took a long sip and tasted chicory—something he hadn't had in his coffee in a long while. "Mmmm," he said. "That's good." The coffee was rich and black and strong.

He pushed a pillow against the headboard, and leaned back to enjoy the view as she went about the business of making a plate for him and then a smaller one for herself. She was as pretty as a night sky, and he felt his manhood stirring once more.

She turned back to him and must have noticed his condition through the thin sheet.

Setting the plates down, she smiled shyly and said, "Do you . . . ?"

He put his coffee on the floor and pulled her into the bed and his arms. "It's the best breakfast in the world," he said.

Pleasuring her, he quickly found, was a pleasure. She was a fast learner and it wasn't long until once again her cries of joy were echoing in the small room.

When they finished, Fargo got his makings out of his saddlebags and rolled himself a smoke, using a saucer as an ashtray. He wanted a bath and suggested they find one.

"I have an idea," she said, sitting up in bed and sipping out of his coffee cup.

"What do you have in mind?" Fargo asked.

"Would you take me for a ride on your horse again,

Skye?" she asked. "I know a place. . . . It's private and we could bathe and do . . . other things."

Fargo laughed. "I think you've developed a taste for sex," he said. "That's a fine quality in a woman as beautiful as you."

She laughed, too, though he could sense her embarrassment. "Please," she said. "I don't want to tire you, but it is beautiful and private." She paused, then added, "And your horse is wonderful. Those colors!"

"He's special," Fargo said. He didn't have anything in particular to do today and a ride away from this place in good company might give him time to think about everything he'd learned—assuming Mary let him think at all. "All right," he said. "We'll go for a ride."

"Thank you!" she squealed. "You won't regret it."

Noticing that in her excitement the sheet had dropped away, Fargo eyed her gorgeous body with appreciation. "I don't reckon I will at that," he said.

Snatching the sheet to cover herself, she giggled again.

"Get yourself dressed," Fargo said.

She jumped out of the bed, ready to head down the street stark naked if it meant getting the day started.

"Then we'll go?" she asked.

Mary was so full of excitement that Fargo couldn't help but join in. "Yes," he said. "Then we'll go."

It didn't take long for them to get Mary outfitted in some comfortable riding clothes and it was only two hours later that they picked up the Ovaro and headed out of the city.

She guided him back to the field where they'd first met and from there to a small grotto nearby. A clear pool had formed beneath the cypress trees and the hanging moss. It was as private as any bathhouse he'd ever been in.

He helped her out of the saddle, then grabbed his soap and a towel from his saddlebags.

The water was almost as warm as she was and it

took quite some time for her to reach all his spots, but with his guidance, they managed to get them all . . . and all of hers, too.

After, she led him to a moss-covered place beneath the trees and they toweled themselves dry. It had been quite a while since Fargo had been with someone of her considerable appetite, but she sat quietly next to him now and let him think.

There was a lot more going on in New Orleans than a simple high-stakes poker game, and more players, he thought, than had actually agreed to come to the table.

With so much at stake, he knew he'd have to be very careful over the next few days if he was going to get out of the city with the money he'd been promised . . . and his life.

Life was often cheap, he knew. But the kind of money and power that was involved in this game was more than enough for many people to kill for. These two jobs—keeping the game fair and keeping Hattie Hamilton safe during the game—wouldn't be easy, lay-down jobs.

They'd be the kind of jobs that could get a lot of men killed. One easy distraction and . . .

Fargo sat bolt upright, realizing that there was a huge distraction sitting next to him. One that had already caused him to lose a night and most of a day.

"Mary," he said, "do you have any family at all around here? Somewhere you could stay for a few days?"

She shook her head. "No. They all been killed or run off during the war. I'm all I got."

Fargo sighed. He'd have to find somewhere to stash her. One look at her eyes or her body and like any man, he could be distracted at a critical moment that could lead to his death. "Well, you've got me," he said. "At least until we figure out what to do."

She smiled and Fargo couldn't help but wonder if he was being played for a fool. He looked into her eyes, but there wasn't the smallest hint of guile. She was innocent, he thought. There wasn't any sign that she was anything other than a beautiful prostitute who'd been caught up in the games of her employer.

Knowing they'd have to head back soon, he put an arm around her and she snuggled close.

There are worse forms of payment in the world, he thought, looking at her. *A lot worse.*

9

H.D. was not happy. In fact, he sounded downright *unhappy*. "Come on, Fargo, I've got better things to do than babysit a whore, for God's sake!"

"Not for the next few days, you don't," Fargo said. "Unless I miss my guess, Parker, Beares, and Anderson are going to pull all their men in and wait for the outcome of the game. It should be pretty quiet around here."

"But why a *whore*, Fargo? My wife will tan my hide and stake it to the front door. Couldn't you have found some nice girl to rescue?"

Fargo chuckled. "I'm not all that big on nice girls," he said. "Mary is special, H.D., and she needs help. I can't watch out for her while dealing with all these other snakes, too."

Fargo could go sentimental and say that there were whores of the body and whores of the heart. Some "nice" girls harbored attitudes about people that were anything but nice. And some whores harbored thoughts that were downright charitable when it came to helping men in and out of bed. As far as Fargo was concerned, that was one of the problems with this world. The poor had to scramble just to get meals sometimes, and this kind of scrambling made them seem coarse to those more prosperous. But the fancy manners of the rich folks would soon be pitched out the window if they, too, had to scramble to put food on the table. And a whole lot of those "nice" girls wouldn't seem so nice anymore, either.

H.D.'s shoulders sagged and Fargo knew the man

had given in. "Don't worry on it too much," he said. "Your wife will understand a woman needing protection, no matter what she does for a living."

His face in his hands, H.D. said, "She'll kill me, Fargo, the second she finds out. She'll think I've been seeing a sporting lady and now I've brought her into our home."

"No, she won't," Fargo said. "What kind of an idiot does she take you for? No sane man would bring his mistress—even a paid one—into the same house as his wife. One woman is trouble enough, let alone two."

"You'd probably know, Fargo," H.D. said. He held up his hands. "Fine, fine. I'll figure it out. When are you coming back for her?"

"Thursday, depending on how fast the game runs. Maybe Friday. Just keep her out of sight until I return."

Throughout this conversation, Mary had remained silent, but Fargo could see she was all but busting at the seams to say something. "What is it, Mary?"

"I don't want to stay with him, Skye. I want to . . . stay with you," she said. "Miz Hamilton told me that's what I was supposed to do."

Fargo shook his head. "Mary, you can't. This poker game is liable to get downright dangerous. I can't do what I have to do if I'm worried about you. You'll be safe with H.D. He's a good man."

"But what if something happens to you?"

H.D. laughed. "Girl, that man you're talking to is the Trailsman. There's no one in New Orleans more dangerous than he is."

Mary looked confused. "He does not seem dangerous to me."

"That's because you haven't tried to kill him," H.D. said. "Yet."

"What do you mean, 'yet'?" Fargo asked.

H.D. grinned evilly. "You just haven't had a chance to piss her off yet, Fargo. Sooner or later, you will, and she'll come at you with a pigsticker and try to gut you like a winter hog. You aren't the kind of man to settle down, my friend. Too many trails yet to ride. Women, in my experience, just hate that."

"You . . . you will be leaving?" Mary asked.

Ignoring his urge to strangle H.D., Fargo said, "Not anytime real soon."

She sagged in relief. "I don't want you to leave, Skye. Not ever."

Another one that wants me to settle down, Fargo thought. *Why can't women just enjoy the time and move on?* "I guess we'll see what happens," he said, then turned his attention back to his meddlesome friend, who was grinning openly. "Thanks," Fargo said drily. "You sure know how to help a man out."

"Least I could do, Fargo," H.D. said. "Given the 'favor' you're doing me."

Unable to help himself, Fargo chuckled. "Fair enough," he said. "Just keep an eye on her. I'll be back as soon as I can."

"All right," H.D. said. He stood up from behind his desk and buckled on his gun belt. "Come on, Mary. I'll show you to where you'll be staying. You'll like my wife. She's a fine woman, a good cook, and she'll fill your head clean full of ideas on how to hog-tie this fella you've set your cap for."

"Great," Fargo said. "Maybe I should have left her in the swamp."

"Naw," H.D. said, "then she'd have ended up taking lessons from the alligators. They know even more evil tricks than my wife."

Fargo clasped Mary in his arms and planted a kiss on her lips. "I'll be back for you in a day or two. In the meantime, listen to what H.D. tells you and stay out of sight."

"You . . . Skye, you promise you'll come back for me?"

Fargo nodded. "I promise. Now get going." He gave her a playful swat on the backside and nodded to H.D. in thanks, then turned and left the office.

He had some scouting to do before the game started. Even in the city, there were trails to follow for a man with the eyes to see them.

If there was such a thing as the crown jewel of a place as seedy as Basin Street, the Blue Emporium was it. No matter what trail he could find, all of them would lead, he suspected, to this one building.

From the outside, it didn't look like much. The building itself was wedged between two others, and was four stories tall. Made of a dark red brick stained with soot, a quick glance would tell a passerby that it was nothing more than a hotel or perhaps a boarding-house. But there were clues that it was something more.

The concrete steps led up to a set of double doors, which were carved of mahogany. On either side of the doors, a sculpture of a scantily clad nymph in a sea-shell welcomed those who approached. Leaded-glass panes decorated each door, and farther up, the obser-vant man would notice that the windows themselves were not cheap glass, but well made, and with nice curtains offering privacy to each room. Small balcon-ies, large enough for a single person and made of wrought iron that was bolted directly into the brick, stuck out from each window.

Fargo had heard that during certain times of the year, when there were citywide parties and festivals, the women would stand on the balconies showing off their "wares" and throwing trinkets of beads to the crowds below. If it was true, he wondered what the typical farmer's wife attending the harvest dance out on the frontier would make of such an activity. He laughed to himself. She'd probably call it the work of the devil.

He walked up the front steps and opened the doors, closing them softly behind him. It was early in the day, and the building was quiet. As he had suspected, the inside was even more luxurious than the outside. The foyer was white and blue marble, with twin pillars setting off the entryway. Beneath his feet, tiny tiles made a picture of yet another nymph, her finger beck-oning suggestively.

Beyond the foyer and to both the left and the right were small sitting rooms. The floors were covered in thick carpets dyed crimson, and the furniture—overstuffed couches and chairs with fat pillows—were a rich golden color. The walls were dark wood and both rooms sported small bars, topped with glass decanters filled with presumably the finest liquor available. Behind each bar, a selection of cigars and other tobacco was available. Carpeted stairways led to both upper and lower floors. Fargo could hear a voice coming from somewhere behind the stairs.

The kitchen, Fargo realized, *must be on this floor, behind the two sitting rooms.* The thought had no sooner crossed his mind when he heard the sound of a familiar voice. He stepped into the sitting room to his right just in time to see Hattie Hamilton enter the room from a recessed doorway in the back.

"Why, if it isn't Skye Fargo," she said. "Welcome to the Blue Emporium." She wore a paisley-print dress that was made of silk and clung to her body as though it had been painted on. Her hair was done up in a neat set of curls that were tied in a bun. As always, her voice and her eyes, even her mannerisms, screamed of a sensual, wanton woman.

"Miss Hamilton," Fargo said.

"I'm sorry I wasn't out here to greet you properly, Mr. Fargo," Hattie said, stepping forward and holding out her hand as though she expected him to shake it or kiss it. "We don't usually get much business at this hour."

"I don't imagine," Fargo said. "I was hoping I could take a look around, if you don't mind, before the game starts."

"Of course, of course," she said. "Can I offer you a cup of coffee? Matilda just brewed some up fresh. There's breakfast, too, if you want it."

"That would be fine," Fargo said. "So long as I can have it in the back. I'm not dressed properly for such a fancy place."

"I had you figured for a backdoor man," Hattie

said, her voice dripping with suggestion, which Fargo chose to ignore. "Right this way."

He followed her out of the parlor, through the recessed doorway, and into the kitchen. It was surprisingly large, but Fargo figured that they probably made a lot of meals here—both for the girls and for the men who frequented the place. A massive black woman was standing over a stove, wielding a whisk in one hand. The smells of sizzling ham, scrambled eggs, and fresh-grated cheese issued forth from a cast-iron skillet big enough to feed a small army.

Hattie led him to a small table and set down a mug, which she filled with coffee. "Black?" she asked.

Fargo nodded and picked up the mug. Like the other coffee he'd had in the city, this one was rich and dark and tasted of chicory. It wasn't something he'd want all the time, but it was a good flavor. He took another sip and said, "That's good. Thank you."

Hattie smiled. "My Matilda brews the best chicory coffee in the city, but wait until you eat her cooking. You'll think you've died and woke up in your mama's kitchen."

"Then she's probably damn handy to have around."

Hattie took a seat at the table, pouring herself a cup of coffee as well. "Matilda says the girls come here for the money but they stay for the food. She may be right," she admitted, smiling. "Of course, they all work up quite an appetite."

Hattie laughed, and Fargo realized that her charms—so noticeable on the docks and at Beares' house—weren't quite as effective as before. He'd been wondering since he'd met her who she reminded him of and he finally figured it out: she was like one of those snake-oil salesmen that came out to the frontier with bottles of pure grain alcohol flavored with a little molasses or ginger or whatever, selling a supposed cure-all for a dollar a bottle. She was, in other words, a woman who would lie, cheat, or do whatever else came to mind or hand, in order to make a buck.

Matilda set a plate in front of Fargo heaped with scrambled eggs, ham and cheese, and two slices of buttered toast.

Fargo chuckled. "I think that'll do it—maybe for a couple of days." He picked up a fork and set to work, his hands busy even as he observed Hattie eating her own breakfast, which consisted of a very small plate of the scrambled eggs and toast.

In between bites, he said, "You don't eat enough to keep a hummingbird alive."

She smiled. "I can't afford to overindulge in food, Mr. Fargo. Most men prefer their women on the slender side."

Fargo finished his plate, filled to bursting, then refilled his coffee cup from the pot on the table. Hattie was done long before he was, but she watched him with the eyes of a happy cat who'd found a mouse to play with. There was something, he knew, deeply wrong with the woman.

When he'd finished his coffee, she took a small ashtray off the shelf and set it on the table. Fargo rolled himself a smoke, and struck a match with his thumb, sighing in satisfaction. "A damn fine breakfast," he said. "Thank you."

Hattie laughed. "I don't imagine you've had much time to eat in the last day or so," she said. "Fleur is an exuberant young lady." She rolled a smoke of her own, lit it, and said, "Where is my little chocolate flower, anyway?"

"Oh, I've arranged for her to be kept busy for the next couple of days," Fargo said. "I want to be sure that my distractions during the game are kept to a minimum."

"I'm sure," Hattie said, sounding a little annoyed by Fargo's answer. "You should have her come by, pick up her things."

"I can bring them to her, but she's got everything she needs," he said. "She won't be coming back."

Hattie laughed again; this time the sound was cruel. "Excuse me, Fargo," she said. "I've heard that one

94

about a million times. You'll tire of her, eventually, and she'll come back. They always do. That's one of the things that keeps me in business—I never lack for girls willing to work."

"I don't suppose," Fargo said, crushing out his cigarette in the ashtray. "I appreciate the breakfast, but the reason I'm here is business."

"Fleur isn't enough to keep you satisfied?" Hattie asked. "I'm amazed."

Fargo shook his head. If the woman could turn the conversation to sex, she did. "No," he said. "The business of the poker game. I'd like to see the room where it will be played."

"Certainly," Hattie said, rising to her feet. "Matilda, will you see to it that the girls get breakfast and ready for the day? You know they'll sleep half the day through if we don't get them going."

"Yes, ma'am, Miz Hamilton," Matilda said.

"Follow me, Fargo," Hattie said, heading back out into the sitting room.

He followed and she led him back to the front entryway. "The upstairs is where the girls' rooms are," she said. "The sitting rooms are where gentlemen callers can take their ease with a fine cigar and a drink until the girl of their choice is available."

"And the downstairs?" Fargo asked.

"That's where we have . . . other rooms," Hattie said. "Come along and I'll show you."

Fargo followed her down the stairs, moving slowly so that she could light the gas lamps ensconced on the walls. The stairs were steep and they went down two flights before coming to a long hallway that branched in either direction.

"These rooms are where we do special entertainments," Hattie said. "To the left, we have rooms for almost any kind of sexual activity you can imagine. And probably a few you wouldn't want to."

Curious despite himself, Fargo said, "I've got quite an imagination."

She patted his arm and once again that surge of

heat passed over him. "I'm sure you do," she laughed. "And that's enough about that."

"I get the picture," Fargo said. Some things were better left unexplored. "And the rooms to the right?"

"Mostly private party rooms. We aren't supposed to allow gambling, but the city looks the other way so long as we keep the officials bribed—and let them play, of course. Every major politician in Louisiana has been down here drinking the best booze found anywhere and playing poker or faro, dealt by a beautiful woman wearing nothing but a smile." Her voice was proud. "I make almost as much money off those rooms as I do the rest of the property combined."

"What's the house take?" he asked.

"Twenty percent," Hattie said. "It adds up fast."

"I'm sure," Fargo said. "Can I see the room where the poker game I'm supposed to be watching is going to be held?"

"This way," she said, turning down the hall to the right and stopping at the last door. "Here it is. We call this the Midnight Room."

She opened the door and the name became self-explanatory. The walls were covered in a wood so dark that it was almost black. In one corner, a fully stocked bar and a case of cigars was almost invisible except for the twinkle of light reflecting off the decanters. Heavy chairs, raised up higher and made of black-dyed leather, were spaced around the walls for those who were observing the table in the center of the room.

The poker table itself was crafted of the same dark, polished wood as the walls, the top covered in flawless green felt. Six wooden containers were situated in the middle of the table, each one filled with chips. Around the table, six comfortable chairs were placed evenly apart, with a seventh chair for the dealer. Crystal ashtrays, cleaned and polished, waited to be used. Everything appeared to be in readiness for the big game.

"It's quite nice, yes?" Hattie said.

"A poker room fit for a king," Fargo replied. His

eyes scanned the room once more. "Is this door the only way in or out?"

"Yes," Hattie said. She walked over to the bar area and moved aside a small curtain. "There is a dumbwaiter here, so that food can be sent down directly from the kitchen, but as you can see"—she slid open the panel that revealed the space—"this isn't large enough for anything other than a few plates stacked on a tray."

Fargo nodded. "I want one of the viewing chairs moved," he said. "Do you mind?"

"Whatever you feel will assist you in your jobs," Hattie said.

"Where will you be during the game?" he asked.

"Behind the bar," she said. "For the most part, anyway. I will have to go upstairs from time to time to check on things, but by the time the game starts, the rest of the house should be fairly quiet."

Looking the room over once more, Fargo reached a decision. The poker table was in the center of the room, the bar area behind it and to the right in one corner. He walked across the room and lifted one of the heavy chairs, placing it several feet behind the dealer's chair—in between the table and the bar. It put him too far from the door for his liking, but there was no helping it. If he was going to both watch the game and protect Hattie, he'd have to be positioned right there.

"This ought to do it," he said.

"Very well," she said. "Is there anything else I can do for you, Fargo? Anything at all?"

The words were suggestive enough, but considering that she was already sleeping with two senators, Fargo figured he'd be better off sticking to business. "Just one more question," he said.

"Of course," Hattie replied, leading him out of the room and back up the stairs. She blew out the gas lamps as they went and Fargo did his best to keep his mind focused on what he needed to know, rather than the seductive sway of her backside through the silk of her gown.

They reached the top of the stairs and paused in the entryway. "You had a question?" she said.

"Yes," Fargo said. "I understand the stakes and the players. I know what I'm supposed to be doing. There's just one piece of information I don't have yet."

"And that is?"

"Who is going to be dealing the cards?" Fargo asked.

Hattie burst out laughing, her voice echoing off the marble entryway in genuine mirth. "Oh, my," she said. "I am truly amazed." She wiped tears away from the corners of her eyes, still laughing. "It hadn't even occurred to me that you didn't know."

"So?" Fargo asked, irritated at her mirth. "Who's dealing?"

"I'm sorry," she said. "I really did think you knew." She managed to get her laughter under control, making a small handkerchief disappear into a sleeve. "I would've thought he would have told you."

"He who?" Fargo snapped.

"Your friend," Hattie said. "John H. D. Timmons will be dealing the cards tomorrow night, Fargo."

Stunned, Fargo felt his jaw unhinge and he had to consciously force himself to close his mouth. When he opened it again, all he could mutter was, "Ah, shit."

That was one twist in the trail he hadn't seen coming at all.

10

Fargo left the Blue Emporium in something of a daze, crossing the street and barely avoiding being run over by a carriage. He needed to think and short of leaving the city, the best place to do that would be back in his room at the Bayou, so that's where he headed.

Once he was back in his room, he stretched out on the bed and closed his eyes. He wasn't tired, but his mind was reeling from the implications of H.D. dealing the cards for the game. On the one hand, it was possible that he'd been chosen because he was unbiased. On the other, it was possible that he'd fallen under the influence of one or more of the players of the game—or simply the influence of cold, hard cash—and was somehow involved in one or more of the schemes going on here.

Fargo squeezed the bridge of his nose between his thumb and forefinger, then started massaging his temples. By his count, there were now six poker players, one dealer, and one brothel madam involved in the game. Of those, five were potential problems and at least four had some kind of vested interest in the outcome. He realized he had a headache . . . and that he much preferred the straight decision making of a good fight than all of these shady characters and their secret plans.

A deep feeling of unease settled itself in his gut. The potential for this to turn into a basement bloodbath was pretty high, and he wondered if his initial assessment about the streets being quiet was right. If any of the three men—Parker, Beares, or Anderson—

wanted to make a move, during the poker game might be the best time.

This, coupled with the fact that H.D. hadn't bothered to mention that he was going to be dealing the cards, led Fargo to reach the conclusion that no matter what he did, he was going to be a target for trouble. Someone would want him dead and out of the way *before* the game tonight.

No sooner had this thought crossed his mind than he heard the faint squeak of a floorboard in the hallway outside his door. It could have been a passerby, someone leaving his room, but the noise would have continued on, rather than ceasing.

Fargo slipped the Colt out of its holster, then placed it alongside, almost beneath, his right leg where it would be hard to spot. The door handle to his room rattled briefly and he mentally cursed himself for not bothering to lock the door when he'd come in. Closing his eyes to mere slits, he feigned sleep and waited, hoping the individual wouldn't just shoot him down.

Through his restricted vision, Fargo saw the deep blue color of a pair of jeans and the tan canvas of a duster. Booted footsteps, quiet but noticeable, stopped at the foot of his bed.

Resisting the urge to move, he kept his breathing slow and steady. Until he heard the cold, metallic click of a pistol being cocked.

A deep voice began to say, "Get up, Trailsman," but Fargo was already moving.

He launched himself forward, bringing the Colt to bear with his right hand, while sweeping the man's gun out of the way with his left.

The man's eyes went wide and he managed to say, "Oh, shit, he's awake!" as Fargo jammed the barrel of the Colt against the man's chest.

From the doorway, Fargo saw another man drawing down on him and he knew he didn't have a choice. These men were here to take him away somewhere and kill him and he wasn't about to let that happen.

Leaping off the bed, Fargo shoved the man in

100

front of him toward the door, just as the other man's gun went off. The bullet slammed into the first man, hammering into his back and driving him to his knees.

From the doorway, the second man said, "Oh, damn, Darby," then tried to take aim at Fargo.

The Trailsman wasn't going to give him the chance and he fired the Colt twice, the sound almost deafening in the small room. Darby fell over backward, dead, at almost the same time that his partner pitched into the hallway, crashing into the wall and sliding down. His eyes held the same look of surprise Fargo had seen on so many faces when meeting the reality of their own deaths. So many men who were willing to kill for money seemed to believe that they were immune to the fate they handed out to others. Death came as a cold surprise, but Fargo suspected they ended up in a much warmer place.

Stepping over Darby's still form, he moved to the man in the hallway who was gasping out his last few breaths. "Heard . . . heard . . . you were good," he wheezed.

"Who sent you?" Fargo snapped, kicking the man's gun down the hallway. "Who wanted me dead so badly that they'd send you in broad daylight?"

The man coughed blood and grinned a red smile. "You . . . you've got to know," he managed. "Just . . . about . . . everyone."

Who? Fargo demanded. "Who sent you?"

"To . . . hell . . . with you," the man said; then his breath hitched one last time and he died.

"Damn it!" Fargo snarled, resisting the urge to give the dead man's body a kick. From the bottom of the stairs, he could hear shouting and the rush of steps. He wasn't even going to have time to search the bodies before half of New Orleans was jammed into the hallway trying to see what had happened.

From experience, Fargo knew that the law would already be on its way—there was always someone who ran for the sheriff the minute they heard gunshots. He walked back into his room to wait, reloading the Colt and taking a position by the window.

Ignoring the questions from the people in the hallway who were alternating their queries with exclamations about the two dead men, Fargo kept his silence, watching the street below.

He wasn't particularly surprised when, several minutes later, he spotted H.D. moving down the boardwalk at a fast clip, a crowd at his heels.

Standing framed in the doorway, H.D. whistled softly at the damage, then turned and said, "Show's over, folks. Go on about your business." People began to drift away and H.D. kept his mouth closed until he and Fargo were alone.

"Seems like you've already made friends here," he quipped. "Want to tell me what happened?"

Fargo shrugged and related the story, not embellishing the details. "They must have figured to take me somewhere outside of town and kill me," he said. "Lots of swamps around here to hide a body in."

"You got that right," H.D. said. "Every so often, the tide shifts a bit and the swamp spits up a couple—usually just a few bones that the gators haven't chewed up." He nudged the body on the floor. "This here is Darby Trent. A local thug, does muscle work for anyone who'll pay him when he's not down in Anderson's Café drinking his wages."

He stepped back into the hall and looked at the other man. "I don't know this one," he said.

"They're all the same," Fargo replied. "Men who will kill for a few dollars and the chance to be famous."

"Not much of a way to make a living, if you ask me," H.D. said, stepping back into the room.

"Nope," Fargo replied. "Then again, moonlighting as a poker dealer isn't, either." He moved closer to his old friend. "You want to tell me what's really going on, H.D.?"

"Ah, hell, Fargo," H.D. said. "All three of them

asked me to do it—Parker, Beares, and Anderson. Said they could trust that I would be fair about it and I could stand to make a little extra money, what with feeding a wife and a whore these days."

"Funny," Fargo said. "The man I knew in Kansas wouldn't have spent time with any of these snakes for two bits and a cold beer."

"The man you knew in Kansas was a lot more naive than I am," H.D. said. "There's no law against it and I'm trying to get enough of a nest egg to retire, Fargo. I'm getting too old for this life." He pointed a finger and added, "I notice *you're* working for them."

"I wouldn't be," Fargo said, "if I'd known what I was really getting into. But I accepted the job from Parker and I don't back out of a job once I've taken it on."

"Even when you find out the truth—that your employer is no better than a rattler himself?" he asked.

"I gave my word," he replied. "I'll see it through, but I play fair and always have. What about you, H.D.? You still playing fair?"

His friend leaned against the dresser. "Fair as I can, Fargo," he said, sighing. "I've got to live here, too. You'll move on after this, just like you always do."

Fargo nodded, then said, "So long as you understand the rules, H.D., you'll do all right."

"What rules?" he asked. "I'm just dealing the cards."

"And if I catch you doing more than that," Fargo replied, his voice soft and menacing, "then you might live to wish I hadn't."

H.D. stared at him for a long moment, then nodded. "I've always been a straight shooter, Fargo. I'll deal the cards that way, too."

"Good enough," Fargo said. He looked at the bodies on the ground and added, "Do you want help moving these down to the undertaker?"

H.D. shook his head. "No, we've got street urchins for that. They'll move 'em for two bits each and be glad for the work. The parish will pick up the cost of getting 'em buried if no one comes to claim them."

"How's Mary making out over at your place?" Fargo asked. "She doing okay?"

"Oh, she's fine as frog's hair," H.D. said. "My wife has a new friend." He sighed heavily. "You were right, Fargo. No sane man would have two grown women in his house. They start plotting against you the minute they think you're out of earshot."

Fargo laughed and a sense of relief washed over him. He didn't think H.D. was on the wrong side of things here, which would mean one less man to worry about. "What makes you think," he asked with a grin, "that they wait even that long?"

Once he was back on the street, Fargo got the feeling that he was being watched again. He tried and almost succeeded in convincing himself that this was stupid. The problem wasn't people behind windows noting his every move—the problem was that this was a city where virtually nobody was trustworthy. Usually when he went into a town he found the good folks right away. Not here. New Orleans was a place where there was no such thing as "the common good." Every group you could name had a "common good," meaning that there wasn't much civic cooperation. It was a wonder that New Orleans had bloomed the way it had. Despite his misgivings about the place, Fargo had to admit that it was a magnificent spectacle of a city and that things only promised to get even bigger and bolder here.

Not that he'd stick around to watch.

In the afternoon before the game was scheduled to start, Fargo grabbed a quick bite at the diner next door and watched the street from the window. The blackened catfish filets he was eating were delicious and the slaw and the cornbread were homemade, but his mind wasn't on his food but on the slow-moving groups of men circling the streets around the Blue Emporium and eyeing each other like soldiers getting ready to go to war.

It took almost a half hour, but eventually Fargo

spotted the two men situated on the roof of the brothel and noted that other men had taken up positions in the alleys nearby. If things went badly tonight, a lot of people were going to die. There were too many guns and too many enemies gathered in one place.

He finished his meal and paid the bill, then stepped into the street. Beneath the brim of his hat, he saw that several sets of eyes followed his movements, but no one bothered him as he strolled around several blocks in either direction, counting the number of men that Parker, Beares, and Anderson had sent to keep watch on the brothel.

By the time he'd completed his circuit, Fargo knew that trouble was brewing and it was only a matter of time until it exploded. He remembered how, out on the plains of Nebraska, a summer storm would roll across the prairie in a black and purple line, the clouds churning and bolts of lightning zapping back and forth as it built up strength. When it hit, it did so with a ferociousness unrivaled in nature, and wise men hid in their root cellars until it was over and they could come out and inspect the damage.

No one in this area had that option.

He went back to his room to change into the new clothing he'd purchased earlier in the afternoon. The loose makings of a plan were now firmly set in his mind and some of it meant looking a particular part. Though Fargo didn't consider himself an actor by any means, he knew that in some situations how a man looked was almost as important as what he might do.

In his room, now cleaned but still smelling faintly of gunpowder, he dressed in black denim jeans and a matching black shirt with bone buttons. He slipped on a new pair of boots, also black, that weren't fit for riding a horse for any distance, but had high enough sides that they could easily hide his boot knives. A paisley-patterned vest in a blue so dark it might as well have been black, completed the clothing portion of his outfit, and he topped it off with a new hat he had no intention of keeping when he left the city.

There were towns on the frontier where this kind of hat would get a man called all kinds of names and lead to fights, but here, it would likely fit right in. It was solid black, too, and made of rich felt. It had a gambler's crown and a wide brim that would serve to hide his eyes. The hatband was woven leather braids interspersed with what the merchant claimed were genuine alligator teeth. They certainly looked real enough, anyway.

Finally, Fargo strapped on a new gun belt—another item he planned on getting rid of as soon as he could. This one was a double-holster rig with midthigh tie-downs, and he placed his well-worn Colt in the right-hand side and a new one in the left—the same model, but in much better shape than his trusted companion. His own gun had seen many years of hard use, but he wouldn't trade it for much of anything.

It had saved his life too many times and Fargo saw no reason to switch, despite the constant advertisements of better weapons he saw whenever he passed through a town of any size.

He took a long look in the mirror and saw that he had achieved the effect he was going for. Parker had hired him to keep a poker game fair and Beares had hired him to protect Hattie during the game, but what both men were going to see when they looked at him tonight was a gentleman gambler and gunfighter, more than ready for trouble.

The person in the mirror bore no small resemblance to a man he'd met only once, in a small gambling saloon in Georgia. The man's name had been John Holliday, a dentist by trade, but when he sat at the card table, even someone of Fargo's background realized that they were sitting with a very, very dangerous man.

Fargo didn't know where John Holliday was now, probably still practicing dentistry somewhere, but he did remember something he'd said while they played cards late one night. "There are only three truths at a card table, Mr. Fargo. The money truth, the card truth, and the people truth. Money, sir, is nothing more than some scribbles of ink on paper. So are cards, for that matter. I play people, Mr. Fargo, which is why I am so *very* good at this game."

Fargo fully intended to take John Holliday's words to heart.

Tonight, he would play the people.

And hold on to the hope that he'd get out alive.

Sunset came and went, and Fargo left his room to grab some dinner, then went out to walk the streets one more time. As though the citizens were animals and could sense impending danger, Basin Street had grown extraordinarily quiet. The saloons and gaming parlors and brothels had very few patrons and most of the people he saw were the same men who had been in the street earlier in the day.

After circling the block, Fargo crossed the street and went up the stone steps into the Blue Emporium. The game was scheduled to start in an hour. Hattie Hamilton was sitting in one of the parlor rooms by herself, while in the other, several of the girls laughed and giggled with men from out of town.

Hattie saw him come in and raised a hand in greeting. Fargo had reached one conclusion about all of the events that had led up to this point: the center of them was Hattie Hamilton.

"Why, Mr. Fargo," she said, rising to meet him. "I had no idea that beneath the plain clothes of a frontiersman, such a fine gentleman existed."

Summoning his coldest voice, Fargo said, "In my experience, Miss Hamilton, being a gentleman has damn little to do with your clothing."

Taken a bit aback, she retreated a step, caught herself, then turned to the bar. "Can I get you a drink?"

"Bourbon," Fargo said. He moved over to the bar, and watched as she poured him a stiff shot from one of the decanters. He took it and tasted a sip. It was warm and smooth and very fine, not unlike a good woman. "This is excellent."

"Thank you," she said. "Do you require anything else before the game begins?"

"One of those cigars, if you wouldn't mind," Fargo said, gesturing to the humidor behind the bar. "It's going to be a long night."

"I imagine so," she said. "Do you expect trouble?"

"I *always* expect trouble, Miss Hamilton," he replied. "It's one of the reasons I'm still alive after all these years."

"One of them?" she asked, handing him a house-rolled Cuban that smelled almost as good as it would smoke. "What are the others?"

Fargo slipped the cigar into his vest pocket, saving it for later. Then he took another sip of the bourbon, savoring its burn. "There are lots of them," he said, "but beyond expecting trouble, there's one thing that's made the difference."

"Oh?" she asked.

Remembering the cold grin of John Holliday, Fargo did his best to mimic it and he was pleased at the reaction on her face. "I don't mind killing people," he said, his voice quiet. "In fact, if it means staying alive, I'll kill anyone or anything that crosses my path."

"I . . . I see," she said, trying to recover. "It's good, then, that you will be protecting me tonight, should trouble happen."

Fargo cocked his head in the direction of the doors. "With as many gunmen as I saw outside, I'd be *very* surprised if a whole bunch of folks didn't end up dead tonight," he said. "Let's hope the right ones make it to the undertakers."

"I'll escort you downstairs," she said, moving from behind the bar and heading for the entryway. "Who would be the right ones?" she asked, leading the way down the steps.

Fargo laughed softly. "There are a lot of players in this game, Miss Hamilton," he said. "For your sake, the right ones better be the ones you've been sleeping with. If they aren't, you're going to be out of business—the dead way—before sunrise."

He was surprised when she laughed, too. "Why, Mr. Fargo, what in the world makes you think I'm not sleeping with all of them?"

11

Hattie left him in the poker room, which he had to himself for the time being. She said little else to him, indicating that he could help himself to anything from the bar, and that she would return when all the players were assembled. Fargo nodded his thanks and took a stroll around the room, looking for anything that might help someone cheat or gain some advantage during the game.

He found nothing, and after checking to ensure that the six wooden crates of chips had been counted out equally, he finished off his bourbon, put the glass down on the bar, and took a seat. Fargo had learned patience the hard way, and he knew that tonight his would be tested to its limits.

The silence stretched on for almost an hour, but then the door to the room opened and Hattie walked in. The players, each of them carrying a leather satchel of some kind, followed behind her: Parker, dressed in a conservative suit of charcoal gray; Beares, in a white cotton suit that made him look younger than he actually was; Anderson, dressed more like a saloon keeper in a cream-colored shirt with a thin string tie and dark slacks; and three men that Fargo didn't recognize, who he assumed were the plantation owners. And last, his old friend H.D., the dealer.

"Fargo," Parker called out as they entered the room. "I'm pleased to see you honored our arrangement, though I didn't imagine you would come dressed in such finery. I expected the frontiersman I met on the riverboat."

"I'm a man of my word," Fargo replied, his voice even. Once more, he wanted to adopt the persona of a professional gambler and gunfighter. "I thought I should dress to fit the occasion."

"You look," Anderson said, "like a hired killer."

"Good," Fargo said.

Before any more words could be exchanged, Hattie said, "Gentlemen, why not take your seats and I'll pour us each a drink?"

There was a general murmur of agreement and the men got themselves arranged around the table. While they were doing so, H.D. stopped next to Fargo's chair and leaned in close. "I'm dealing it straight," he whispered. "And I wanted you to know that I sent my wife and Mary out of town." His voice dropped even lower and he added, "If something happens, there's a note beneath my mantle that will tell you where to find them."

"What do you think will happen?" Fargo whispered back.

H.D. shrugged. "Cards, I hope."

"I wouldn't bet on it," he said.

H.D. nodded and took his seat in the dealer's chair. Hattie poured drinks and passed them around, skipping over Fargo when he shook his head. He couldn't afford to be slowed tonight.

Hattie raised her own glass and said, "To poker, gentlemen, and the peaceful resolution of problems."

"Hear, hear," the men said. Everyone drank, Fargo noticed, except Anderson, who raised his glass to his lips and faked it.

"Gentlemen," H.D. said. "This is a fifty-thousand-dollar buy-in game. There will be no buying back in. Once you're out, you're out. The game is five-card draw, nothing is wild, and there is no limit. Mr. Fargo is here to make sure that everyone plays fair, is that understood?"

There was a chorus of agreement. "Fargo, do you have anything you'd like to say before we start?"

Fargo considered this for a moment, then stood up.

"I know three of the men at the table, but I'd like the names of the others."

The men introduced themselves, and no one bothered to shake hands. One of the men, Armand Delgado, was clearly of Spanish origin. One, who introduced himself as Colonel William Bosswaite, was a retired soldier who looked eager to spend his money very quickly. The third, Fargo thought, was probably the sharpest of the three.

"Aldus Horn," he said. There was a smooth confidence to his voice that told Fargo that he was a man who knew what he was doing, even if he didn't understand the true stakes of the game.

"Good," Fargo said. He moved his gaze from man to man, then said, "I noted a very large number of armed men in the immediate vicinity of the Blue Emporium before I came in tonight, gentlemen. I want each of you to understand something very clearly: should one of you decide that the best way to win this game is to stage some sort of raid on this place, using force, I won't ask who is responsible."

He smoothly drew the Colt from his right holster, the motion so fast that several men blinked in surprise. "I will assume *all* of you are responsible and ensure that at the least, you are held accountable. Is that clear?"

Another chorus of agreement, then Fargo sat down and added, "Play fair, gentlemen. I will be watching."

"Very good," H.D. said. He turned his attention back to the players. "Gentlemen, please put your buy-in money on the table. I will count it and give you your chips. The money will be held in plain sight on the bar."

The men began to pony up the money, and even Fargo felt himself a little amazed. There was three hundred thousand dollars on the table—in cash—and not one of the men was even sweating. It was enough money to buy entire provinces in Mexico.

And more than enough to kill for.

Fargo helped H.D. move the money to the bar once

it had all been counted, then sat back down in his chair to watch the real game begin.

In the beginning, everyone played conservatively. There were no huge raises, no one leaped to call bluffs, and the stacks of chips ebbed and flowed like a sluggish creek. They were two hours into the game when H.D. called for a break.

Everyone agreed and got to their feet. Hattie signaled Matilda and the dumbwaiter was sent down with several platters of food, including meat, bread, and cheese for those who wanted to make themselves a sandwich. Fargo ignored the food, but did get a cup of coffee.

Several of the men used the restroom down the hall and returned. The players' voices were serious and quiet. A visual check showed that the piles of chips were still pretty even, though Aldus Horn had a slight lead. He didn't bluff, Fargo had noticed.

After the break, everyone sat back down, and he noticed that all the men were slightly more intense, as though the first two hours of play had merely been a way to gauge the other players. Several hands were played at much the same pace, and then Armand Delgado took his five cards and made a fairly large bet.

"Five thousand," he said, putting the chips into the pot.

To his left, Horn immediately folded. "No, thanks," he said.

Colonel Bosswaite stared at his cards for a long minute, then looked at Delgado. "Call," he said, adding his own chips to the pot. With the hundred-dollar antes, there was now ten thousand, six hundred dollars' worth of chips in the middle of the table.

"Interesting," Parker said. "Why don't I believe you, Delgado? Is it because you're a bluffer and you always have been or is it, do you think, just because you're a loser who happened into some money?"

Delgado's eyes sparked but he kept his silence.

"Call," Parker said. "And raise another ten thousand." He put the chips in the pot.

"Damn," Anderson said. "I fold."

"You've got more mouth than anything else, Parker," Beares said. "But in this case, I agree." He slid a large stack of his own chips forward. "Call."

"I call," Delgado said, adding chips to the table.

H.D. was a little wide-eyed as he said, "Cards, gentlemen?"

"One," Delgado said.

H.D. slid the card to him. "Senator Parker?"

Parker was silent, then said, "I'll stand pat."

Anderson whistled. "Hope you've got a good hand, amigo. There's over fifty thousand dollars sitting there."

"Senator Beares?" H.D. said.

"Two," Beares replied, his voice steady.

"Your bets, gentlemen," H.D. said, his voice cracking. There was more money riding on this one hand than he'd see in two lifetimes. "And, Hattie, can I have a glass of water, please?"

She brought him the water.

Fargo watched as Delgado sorted through his stack, counting his remaining chips, then moved them forward. "I'm all in," he said. "For another twenty-eight thousand."

Parker looked over his stack. If he called and lost, he more than likely wouldn't have enough money to last even another hour. "Check," he said, obviously wanting to see what Beares would do.

Senator Beares was in much the same position, but he didn't hesitate. "Call," he said, moving all but perhaps a couple of thousand dollars into the middle of the table. "You don't have it."

"Senator Parker?" H.D. said. "Your bet, sir."

Parker was silent for a long moment, then shook his head. "I fold."

H.D. took a long swallow of water, then said, "Your cards, gentlemen."

Delgado smiled, and laid his hand out one card at

a time: ten of hearts, ten of clubs, ten of diamonds, jack of hearts, jack of spades. "Full house," he said. "Tens full of jacks."

Beares' expression never changed. "A nice hand, Mr. Delgado. Very nice."

Delgado started to reach for the pot, but Beares' voice stopped him. "Perhaps, however, you should look at mine before you decide you've won." He put all five of his cards down on the table. Four queens with an ace kicker.

"Four of a kind," Beares said, "always beats a full house."

"You . . . you drew that!" Delgado accused. He turned his eyes on H.D. "You're dealing to him!"

H.D. held up his hands. "I just deal the cards, Mr. Delgado. Straight and fair."

"Mentiroso!" Delgado said, calling H.D. a liar. *"Tramposo!"* he added to Beares, calling him a cheat.

Fargo stood up. "The hand was fair, Delgado," he said. "You just got outplayed. Sit down and finish the game or walk away, but in either case, shut up."

Delgado snarled several more invectives and began to sit down, but Fargo knew better. As Delgado bent his knees, he also went for the gun he wore in a reverse rig under his shoulder.

Fargo wasn't sure who Delgado was going to shoot and didn't care. The Colt was out of its holster in a blink and he put a round through Delgado's outstretched gun hand. The bullet passed through his palm and into his ribs, knocking him over backward. His unused gun fell to the floor with a clatter.

Moving forward, Fargo picked up the gun and tucked it in his belt, then looked down at the wounded man. "You won't die from that wound," he said. "But you probably should get yourself to the doctor real quick."

Delgado struggled to his feet, seething with rage. Fargo knew that if the man had another weapon, he'd have tried to use it. "I have heard of you, Senor

Fargo," he said. "Before I came to Louisiana, your name was mentioned quite a lot near the border. The Trailsman. Some say you are nothing but a hired gun; others say worse. I will make sure that word of this gets back there, as well."

Fargo nudged his wounded ribs with the barrel of the Colt and Delgado cursed. "I bet you will," he said. "You just want to remember that words and actions both have a way of coming back to haunt a man. You don't want me on your trail, Delgado. Now get out of here. You're done."

Delgado stared at him a moment more, then nodded. "Yes," he said. "I am done." He started to reach for the last of his chips on the table.

"Leave them!" Fargo barked. "Once you pay in, that's it. The money stays in play."

"Hijo de puta," Delgado said.

"You're not the first one to say so," Fargo said. He gestured with the Colt. "Don't make me ask you again."

Delgado spun on his heel, slamming the door shut behind him.

The room was deathly silent; then H.D. said, "Fargo, is there anyone you meet that you don't shoot?"

Everyone broke out laughing at once, and then Parker said, "Come on, gents. We've got a game going here."

For a man who'd just lost fifteen thousand dollars, he seemed to be in a pretty good mood. And Beares was almost euphoric as he stacked up his winnings. He now had a substantial lead.

The last of Delgado's chips were divided up equally among the players, and Fargo reloaded the Colt and sat back down as the game resumed with the five remaining players.

Once more, several hands passed in calm and then the colonel made a move after the draw. He took two cards, and when the bets came around again, he said, "Twenty thousand."

"Colonel, you must have gotten the cards you

wanted," Horn said. He'd taken three cards. "But I'll call, anyway."

Fargo knew why. The colonel was the only man at the table who was perspiring. He was bluffing and if Fargo could recognize it, then the others likely could, too. Parker did, and called immediately. Anderson folded, as did Beares.

Neither of them, Fargo assumed, had a hand, or both would have played.

"Cards, gentlemen?" H.D. said.

The colonel was sweating like a pig as he turned over his two pair, eights and aces.

Horn laughed. "Not even close," he said. He turned his own cards over. "Three nines."

Parker chuckled softly. "Thought you might have had me, Horn," he said. "But not while I'm holding a straight." He laid out the cards: six, seven, eight, nine, and ten.

Horn frowned but said nothing, while the colonel swore under his breath. Parker raked in a large pot and now shared the lead with Beares.

Anderson, Fargo noted, had been folding most of his hands early, winning small pots now and again, and losing very little. Horn had been playing well until he'd convinced himself that beating the colonel meant winning the hand. He'd have to make up ground quick to stay in it.

The colonel was all but done and he knew it.

On the next hand, he went all in for his last few thousand and lost it to Anderson, who seized on the opportunity afforded him by three-of-a-kind jacks. Unlike Delgado, however, the colonel appeared to take his loss in stride and he shrugged. "Ah, well, gentlemen. It's only money, right?"

"Of course," Parker said. "Which is why you spend it so freely."

The colonel laughed. "Senator, I've been wealthy and I've been dirt poor. I prefer being rich—and I am—but I know what truly matters in this world. Do you?"

"I wouldn't be a senator if I didn't," Parker snapped, disliking the implied insult. "I was elected because I take care of the people in my parish, and look to their needs."

The colonel laughed. "Oh, bullshit," he said. "You got elected because you had your men stuff ballot boxes like they were Thanksgiving turkeys."

Parker's face reddened and he started to rise. Fargo got to his feet. "Sit down, Senator," he said. "The colonel is leaving." He paused, then added, "Aren't you, sir?"

The colonel nodded. "Indeed, Mr. Fargo." He tipped his hat to the others. "Good night and good luck, gentlemen."

He turned and left the room.

"He took that well," Anderson said. "All considered."

"What do you mean by that?" Horn asked.

"He's not wealthy," Anderson replied. "He's broke. His plantation will be on the market by tomorrow afternoon and if he's lucky, he'll make enough to clear his debt and maybe start over somewhere else."

"How do you know that?" Horn asked.

Anderson smiled. "Because I'm the one he owes money to," he said.

"How much?" H.D. asked, his curiosity getting the better of his usually quiet nature.

"Enough," Anderson said, "that even if I lose tonight, I can always start building a new Storyville somewhere else. I understand that the weather in California is most agreeable."

"Another liar," Beares said. "If you had that much, you wouldn't be here tonight, playing for the stakes we've agreed on."

Anderson put his next ante in the middle of the table and didn't bother to reply. He simply looked at H.D. and said, "Let's keep going, shall we?"

They were almost four hours into the game and had lost two players. The ones remaining, Fargo knew, would last quite a bit longer and he settled himself in for a long night of watching. So far, no one had been cheating that he could see.

Hattie refilled everyone's drinks, then took up her station behind the bar for another half hour before she said, "Gentlemen, if you'll excuse me, I need to check on the girls upstairs."

"Of course," Parker said, getting to his feet. "We aren't going anywhere."

"Should we take a break?" Beares asked, also rising. "Until you return?"

"Come on," Anderson snapped. "We don't need a woman here to play cards, do we? Let's keep this thing moving along."

"Whatever you say, *Mayor*," Beares snapped. "I suggest we take a break." He looked at the others for support and saw none forthcoming.

"Well, to hell with it," he said. "I'm taking a damn break. Come along, Hattie. I'll escort you upstairs."

It finally seemed to sink in to Parker what Beares really wanted to take a break for and he said, "I think I'll come along, too. I could use some fresh air."

"I'm stunned," Anderson said, laughing. "It's taken this long for the two of you to figure out that you're both sleeping with that woman?"

"I am not!" Beares stammered. "How dare you accuse—"

"I'll dare whatever the hell I want," Anderson interrupted. "You two want to fight over Basin Street and Storyville. I built them up from nothing. But I wasn't being led around by the balls while I was doing it."

Hattie whistled sharply, already at the door. "This is a pointless argument, gentlemen," she said. "Since I won't be bedding anyone tonight."

"And that," H.D. muttered under his breath, "truly is a shame."

Hattie, Parker, and Beares headed upstairs, while Anderson and H.D. sat and smoked.

Fargo stayed put for several minutes, then he moved to stand next to H.D. "Can you keep an eye on things here for a few minutes?"

"Why's that?" H.D. asked.

"Just a feeling—" Fargo started to say, when the sound of gunshots echoed through the building. "Ah, damn it to hell," he said, running from the room and wondering which of the men was dead.

12

The acrid smell of gunpowder still hung in the air when Fargo reached the top of the steps, with H.D. and Anderson hot on his heels. The front door of the Blue Emporium was standing open, and lying face-down in a pool of his own blood was Senator Beares.

Hattie was standing over the body, her back to the stairs and a small pistol in her hand, while Parker stood next to the door, his mouth hanging open in shock.

"What the hell happened up here?" Fargo demanded.

Hattie spun toward him, and he quickly reached out and disarmed her. A woman with a gun was a danger-ous thing in almost any circumstance, which Fargo knew from hard-won experience.

H.D. took the pistol from Fargo's hand and de-manded his own explanation.

"I didn't kill him, if that's what you're suggesting," Hattie snapped.

"I hadn't suggested it yet," H.D. said. "But you are the one standing here with a gun and Senator Beares looks pretty dead to me."

"She didn't do it," Parker said. "We . . . Beares opened the door and there was someone standing on the steps, waiting for him. He shot Beares and Hattie pulled out her pistol and fired back, but the villain had already fled down the steps and into the street."

Fargo stepped over Beares' body and looked out on the street, where curiosity about the shot was bringing people outside. He scanned the crowd, but the dark made most of the faces virtually anonymous. He knelt down on the steps, looking for any traces of blood. "There's no sign here," he said to H.D. "No blood except for Beares'."

"Hattie," H.D. said. "I've got to take you in for questioning and send a couple of men over to pick up Senator Beares' body."

"Questioning?" Hattie snapped. "Why? Senator Parker just vouched for me."

"I'm aware of your relationship with Senator Parker," H.D. said. "And it makes sense that he'd want to protect you—and his investment in the Blue Emporium. You need to come with me."

"This . . . this is outrageous!" Hattie screeched. "Why would I kill Senator Beares?"

"I don't know," H.D. said. "But you can tell me all the reasons you wouldn't down at the jail."

"Is this absolutely necessary?" Parker demanded. "We have a game to finish."

"Not really," Anderson said, coming up the stairs for a second time.

"What do you mean by that?" Parker asked.

"Horn is gone," Anderson said. "And so is our money."

"Game called on account of murder," Fargo said. "Perfect."

"Why are you up here, Fargo?" the senator asked. "*You* were supposed to be downstairs watching over our money."

"No, Senator," Fargo said. "I was supposed to be watching the players, remember? That's what you hired me for. When the players split up, I had to make a choice. I chose to stay downstairs until the shooting started up here."

"Damn it all to hell!" Parker shouted. He stepped outside and walked down the steps. "Michaels, Douglas! Get over here!"

Two men drifted in from the crowd and Parker spoke rapidly to them, no doubt sending them out to search for Horn and the missing money. He came back up the steps and said, "They'll find him."

"I wouldn't bet on it," Fargo said. "All of this, I think, was pretty well planned." He turned to Hattie. "Wasn't it, Miss Hamilton?"

"I don't have any idea what you're talking about!" she snapped.

"Why don't you take her away now, H.D.?" Fargo suggested. "I'll come by in a bit and see if I can help you shed some light on this mess."

"You do that, Fargo," he said. He took Hattie by the arm and began walking her down the steps. Her voice rose to a screeching protest that faded as he moved her down the street at a rapid walk.

"What are you going to do now, Fargo?" Anderson asked.

"What I do best," Fargo replied. "I'm going to find Horn."

"This isn't the wilderness, Fargo," Senator Parker said. "There are no tracks in the dust for you to follow."

"I don't quit that easily, Senator Parker," Fargo said. "I'll find him and bring him back."

"Just make sure you don't lose your way," he said. "With all our money."

Anderson chuckled grimly. "I think maybe you hired the wrong kind of man, Parker," he said. "Fargo doesn't strike me as the kind of fellow who would do such a thing."

"Maybe," the senator admitted. "But it's more likely that my men will find him first."

"And then where will our money go?" Anderson asked. "And that doesn't even begin to address the true stakes we were playing for."

"No, it doesn't, does it?" Parker replied. "Perhaps we'll have to work out another arrangement later."

"This is my part of town," Anderson said. "If you want it, you'll either win it or take it by force. But I'll be damned if I'm going to give it to you just because you threaten me."

"You're fighting a losing battle, Anderson," he replied. "Sooner or later, all of this will belong to me."

"I guess we'll see, won't we?"

"That's enough," Fargo said. "I'm not going to stand here all night while you two work yourselves up to a fight. Go on back to your places and I'll get to work."

Parker waved a hand dismissively. "Whatever you say, Fargo. Just be sure that if you do find Horn, you come back with our money."

Anderson didn't speak, just turned and stalked out into the night. Several men fell in next to him as he moved down the street, and Fargo watched long enough to make sure they were gone, then waited until Parker, too, found some men to bring up his carriage and drive him back to his mansion. Inwardly seething, Fargo started into the warren of streets surrounding the Blue Emporium.

Somehow, Horn had slipped out with a lot of money and half the thugs in the city would be on his trail. But Fargo knew that sometimes the fastest way to track a man was to follow instinct instead of a trail. He'd meant to play the people tonight, and had been played himself.

It was not a sensation that he enjoyed very much at all, and he was certain that Hattie was mixed up in the whole thing somehow. But before he could prove that, he'd have to catch Horn and get the money that had been stolen.

Worse still, if his suspicions about those involved were correct, he had more enemies right now than Horn himself.

The city streets were quiet once more when, two hours after the shooting, Fargo slid around the back side of the Blue Emporium. He'd wanted to listen to H.D. question Hattie, but his instincts told him that Horn hadn't gone all that far.

Kicking a scavenging rat out of his way, Fargo moved to stand beside the door that led into the kitchen. Inside, Matilda alternately spoke and sang softly to herself. She had a sweet voice that carried long, low notes of melancholy in it. He imagined that working for Hattie Hamilton would do that to most anyone.

After waiting almost a half hour more, he heard Matilda mutter, "Lord God, but that man does like his vittles, don't he?"

As far as Fargo knew, there were no men left inside the Blue Emporium, so he continued to trust his instincts and silently opened the back door and stepped into the shadows that surrounded it. Matilda was standing at the counter, her head wrapped up in a towel of some kind and wearing a housedress that was so large it could have served as a field tent for any two normal-sized soldiers.

She was making a large plate of food, most of it out of the cold storage box set into one wall. Fried chicken, cut-up carrots, and coleslaw covered the plate. She added two cold buttermilk biscuits and a large pat of butter. "That ought to do him," she muttered. "And if it doesn't, he can damn well make more for his own self."

Fargo was considering his options when his instincts tried to scream a warning, but it was too late. He felt the cold steel barrel of a pistol pressed up against the back of his skull.

"You don't want to move, Mr. Fargo," Horn said from behind him. "Not even a twitch until I say so, understood?"

"I understand," Fargo said. "I guessed you were still here."

"You're a good guesser," Horn said. "Or just a bit smarter than the others."

Matilda watched with wide-eyed interest from the kitchen as Horn pushed Fargo into the dimly lit space. "Mr. Horn!" she said. "Why on earth you puttin' a gun to that man's head? I thought you wanted to eat!"

"Sit down, Fargo," Horn said, moving him toward one of the chairs. "Maybe we can talk a bit."

Fargo sat down and finally managed to get a look

at Horn's face. He appeared tired, but his eyes were still watchful. "You don't want my guns?" Fargo asked.

"Not unless I have to have them," Horn said. He sat down heavily in another chair, but kept his gun aimed and ready. "We need to talk."

Matilda set the plate down on the kitchen table next to Horn's elbow and said, "I'm goin' back to my sleep, Mr. Horn. If you need something else, you're already in the kitchen."

"Fair enough," Horn said. "Thank you, Matilda, and good night."

"Good night," she said, heading through a door Fargo hadn't seen which led into the second sitting room, where Horn had been waiting for him.

Once she was gone—her heavy tread making the stairs above their heads creak alarmingly—Horn said, "Good, now we can have a talk without listening to that woman ramble."

"So, talk," Fargo said, wondering where this was leading.

Horn reached inside his coat and pulled out a badge. "The name's not Horn," he said. "It's James McKenna. I'm a Pinkerton agent."

The light dawning, Fargo nodded. "So where's the real Horn?" he asked.

"Dead," McKenna said. "I had hoped to use him to find out more about Parker, Beares, and Anderson, but when I went out to his plantation, I found him in his parlor, dead maybe one or two days. It looked like a heart attack, maybe. He was slumped over his desk, and I guess it's a lucky thing I showed up. All of the money he'd planned on using for this game was in stacks on his desk."

"None of his workers had bothered it?" Fargo asked, amazed.

McKenna laughed. "Apparently, he'd told them not to disturb him, no matter what."

"They took his orders seriously, I take it," he said.

"I'm pretty sure they heard him collapse," Mc-

Kenna said, "and just left him in there to die. Horn wasn't a very nice man, by all accounts."

"How is it that Parker or Beares didn't recognize that you weren't Horn?" Fargo asked. "I assumed they knew him."

"They did," McKenna said, "but only through correspondence. Horn's plantation is up near Lafayette. He was known by reputation to be something of a gambler."

"I'll be damned," Fargo said. He gestured to the gun in McKenna's hand. "How long do you suppose you're going to keep pointing that thing at me?"

"Just one question," McKenna said, "before I put it away."

"What's that?" he asked.

"Are you sleeping with Hattie Hamilton, too?"

"Hell, no," Fargo said. "I prefer my women to be poison free, and she's the kind that might be death in the sack."

"Good," he said, putting the gun back into its holster. "Because then I don't have to shoot you. Before this is done, I imagine I'm going to have to kill every man involved in this who's been sleeping with her."

"Why?" he asked. "How is she wrapped up in all this?"

"Fargo," McKenna said, "if I'm right, Hattie Hamilton isn't just wrapped up in all this—she is the source of all this."

It made a certain amount of sense, Fargo realized, but still it was hard to believe that one Basin Street prostitute could create this much chaos. "How did the Pinkertons get involved?" he asked. "Policing the New Orleans nightlife doesn't seem like something they'd be interested in."

"On the contrary, Fargo, we're very interested in keeping things here just like they are—for now."

"Why?" he asked. "I'm not sure I understand your interest."

McKenna smiled grimly. "Because when the time comes, we're going to make an example of this city to

127

the whole country. But we're going to do it on our terms and right now, that means keeping the status quo."

"An example?" Fargo asked. "What kind of example?"

"This city is going to burn, Fargo, right down to the cobblestones. It's a cesspool of crime and we're going to clean it up and we're going to do it in a way that makes clear to every city in America what can happen if they don't police themselves." McKenna leaned back in his chair and dug into the food Matilda had left for him.

Not quite sure how to respond to this statement, Fargo said, "How'd you get Matilda involved?"

"She's a paid informant," the Pinkerton man said between bites. "It was her that showed me how to escape the basement unseen and she hid me until the commotion died down."

Fargo watched the other man eat in silence for a couple of minutes, his mind churning. If McKenna was telling the truth, a lot of innocent people were going to die. Every city had its good and bad, but the good folks shouldn't be killed along with the bad just to make an example for everyone else.

On the other hand, there was nothing to prove that McKenna was telling the truth. All Fargo had to go on was his badge and he could have gotten that easily enough. It was possible he *was* Horn, or someone else just playing the game to make money for himself.

It seemed like there was no one in this town he could truly trust, so Fargo did the only thing he could. He stood up, trying to appear casual, and stretched. "It sounds like maybe you've got a plan."

McKenna or Horn or whoever he was nodded. "First thing tomorrow, I'll take the money down and put it in the bank to be wired to Chicago—confiscated funds."

"What then?" Fargo asked.

"Then I'll—" was all the man managed to say before the butt end of Fargo's Colt slammed into his head, knocking him unconscious.

"Take a nap," he finished for him. "A good long one."

"At least you didn't shoot this one," H.D. said, looking at the prone form of McKenna on his office floor. "So you found Horn?"

The office was dark and quiet, but morning wasn't all that far off. Fargo shrugged. "Horn, maybe. He told me he was really a Pinkerton agent."

"Christ, Fargo, you clubbed a Pinkerton man? Do you want to be chased from here all the way into the Indian nations?"

"Something about his story didn't ring quite true," he said. He filled H.D. in on what McKenna had told him.

"Burn the city down?" H.D. said. "I don't believe it."

"I don't either," Fargo said. "But who knows what the real truth is? For now, we've got to get him out of town."

"What do you suggest?"

"Can you and your men truss him up and get him on a northbound train?" he asked. "Maybe in a freight car where they won't find him for a while? By the time he gets back, we can hopefully have the rest of this sorted out."

H.D. nodded. "Yeah, I can manage that. But there's something I've got to tell you, Fargo."

"Go ahead."

"I had to let Hattie Hamilton go," H.D. said. "The county attorney showed up about an hour ago. Parker got him out of bed and forced him to come down here. He told me to cut her loose for a 'lack of evidence.' "

"Damn," Fargo said. "I was hoping you'd be able to hold her for at least another couple of days."

"Me, too," he said, "but he was right. We didn't have much in the way of evidence and Parker verified her story."

"Where'd she go?" he asked. "She didn't come

back to the Blue Emporium. That's where I've been most of the night."

"Parker's place, I imagine," H.D. said. "Why?"

"Because I've got the feeling that she really is at the center of all this." He nudged the man on the floor. "Tell you what," he said. "Just lock him up for now and when he comes around, why don't you see if you can get some sort of verification of his story?"

"What are you going to do?" H.D. asked.

"What I always do," Fargo said, turning back to the doorway.

"Do you know who you're after?" H.D. called after him.

"Just about everyone," he replied. "But first things first. I'm going to take that money to the only man I can trust with it."

"You've got the money? Why didn't you say so?"

"Because, my old friend," Fargo said, his voice sounding tired even to himself, "I can't trust you with it."

"What? Why not?"

Fargo stopped in the doorway, not bothering to turn around. "You're sleeping with her, too, aren't you, H.D.?"

The silence behind him was answer enough and he sighed. "You should have stayed out west, H.D. This place isn't good for you."

"Are you . . . you're not going to tell my wife, are you?" he asked. "She'd be heartbroken."

"No, H.D., not unless I find out that you're in this with her. My advice to you is to find a way to get yourself clear of this place. It's no good." He paused, then said, "She's no good."

"I know," H.D. said. "I just . . . I don't know what to do."

"Yes, you do," Fargo said as he stepped out the door and back into the night. "Or at least you used to."

He listened, but his old friend didn't say anything

else, and Fargo realized that more than likely H.D. wasn't someone he could call a friend anymore.

Worse, he might just be an enemy.

Still, he would deal with that when the time came. For now, he had to see a man about holding on to a very large sum of money.

Fargo only hoped that his instincts would prove accurate this time. Any kind of game played in this place was dangerous. But he'd managed to find one that was especially so. He remembered something an old friend of his named Cheyenne had told him once: "There're two things a man'll kill you for right off. Money and a woman. He'll kill you faster for the woman but he'll kill you slower for the money." Fargo reckoned that that was the kind of good advice that would never go out of style. He'd found it true too many times to doubt it.

And without doubt Cheyenne's words applied to a place like this.

13

Fargo headed for Anderson's Café and wasn't all that surprised to find both father and son still awake and discussing the events of the night. The door was locked and he could see them sitting at a table, an oil lamp burning low between them.

He tapped lightly on the door, then stepped away from it. There was no sense in crowding the space and risk getting shot for his trouble. Tommy peered through the window, saw who it was, and opened the door. "Skye Fargo," he said, smiling. "What brings you here at this god-awful hour of the day?"

"Can I come inside for a moment?" Fargo asked.

"Sure, sure," Tommy said. He turned back to where his father was still sitting. "Dad, it's Fargo."

"I heard, boy," Anderson said. "Don't keep him standing in the doorway. Let him in."

Tommy moved aside, then shut and locked the door behind him. "Can't be too careful right now," he said. "Things are a bit unsettled."

Fargo chuckled and crossed over to where Anderson was sitting. "Unsettled is putting it a bit mildly."

"He's got a gift for understatement," Anderson said. "Yet that same mouth lands him in so much trouble."

"He'll grow out of it," Fargo said. "Probably."

"Sit down, Fargo," the man said. "Can I get you something?"

"No, I'm fine," he replied, taking a seat across from the mayor. "But I've come to ask a favor."

Anderson laughed. "I'm on my way to being the

mayor of nowhere and you want a favor? All right, why not? What can I do for you?"

Fargo pulled his saddlebags off his shoulder and tossed them on the table. "I need you to hold these for me, keep them safe until all of this gets figured out."

"What's in them?" Anderson asked.

"About three hundred thousand dollars," Fargo said. "The money from the poker game."

"Thank God!" he exclaimed. "How did you find it? Did you catch Horn? What happened?"

"For a man who didn't seem all that concerned about money during the game, you seem awfully excited to have that money back," Fargo said.

Anderson nodded. "I was bluffing. Even if I get every damn dime I'm owed by people, I wouldn't have enough to rebuild what I've got here. I was laying it all on the line in that game."

"I thought so. You're either really brave or incredibly stupid, Anderson. The game was a setup from the beginning."

"I figured as much, but what else was I going to do except try to win?" the man asked. "Parker and Beares had me cornered."

"Beares is dead," Fargo said evenly, "which gives you one less enemy to deal with. As for Parker, I'm not sure what his role in all this is just yet, but I'll know sooner rather than later."

"What happened to Horn?" the younger Anderson asked.

"He's over in the jail," he replied. "H.D.'s got him locked up nice and tight."

Anderson sighed heavily. "Fargo, I know he was a friend of yours, but H.D. Timmons is as crooked as a dog's hind leg. He's been on Parker's payroll for at least two years."

Fargo absorbed this information in silence, his worst fears about his old friend confirmed. The lure of money had taken him from the side of right and justice. "Are you sure?" he asked. "He's got a wife."

Anderson burst out laughing. "Oh, wow, Fargo, you missed *that* trail, anyway. H.D. doesn't have a wife."

"He doesn't?" Fargo heard himself ask, while his mind raced in another direction. *Where was Mary?*

"No way," the younger Anderson said. "He gets his down at the Blue Emporium, like everyone else on the take around here."

"Ah, shit," Fargo said. "Things just got more complicated."

"What do you mean?" Anderson asked.

Fargo shook his head. "It's not important right now. Can you get that money into a safe and hold it until all this is straightened out?"

The mayor of Storyville nodded. "Sure. You mind if I take out my investment?"

"Go right ahead," he said. "But let's make sure the rest of it stays there. I think we're going to need it later, to square the accounts."

Anderson agreed and gave the saddlebags to his son. "Take this to the vault," he told him. "Count out fifty thousand and set it in my personal drawer. Leave the rest alone."

"Yes, sir," Tommy said, scurrying away.

"Anything else I can do for you, Fargo?" Anderson asked. "It's been a long night and right now, I just want to get some sleep."

"No," he said. "I'll be back later today, hopefully to settle all this once and for all."

"Where are you going now?"

"It's time I had a talk with Senator Parker," Fargo said. "Do you know where his mansion is?"

Anderson gave him the directions and told him the fastest way to get there. "Just watch yourself out there," he added. "Parker's men play for keeps."

"So do I," Fargo replied, getting to his feet.

"You don't lay down very often, do you?" the man asked.

"Not if I can help it," he said.

"You've got sand, anyway," Anderson said. "Stay safe, and when you get back, I'll buy you a drink or four."

"Sounds good," Fargo said, heading for the door. Anderson's voice stopped him.

"How come you brought the money to me?" he asked. "Why did you trust me over your friend H.D., or why not just hold on to the money yourself?"

The Trailsman chuckled quietly. "You were the only one at the table tonight playing for stakes that mattered to you," he said. "Despite your reputation, you actually care what happens to Basin Street and the people who live here. The others just want money and power."

"Thanks," Anderson replied. "Thanks, Fargo."

"Thank me if I live," he said, then unlocked the door and slipped back out into the night once more.

The livery stable was dark, and Fargo didn't bother waking the man on night duty, who was curled up on the hay, hands wrapped around a cheap bottle of rotgut and snoring like a hibernating grizzly. In point of fact, Fargo didn't think the end of the world would wake him up.

He found his saddle and tack on a rack outside the Ovaro's stall, and when he opened the gate to let the horse out, it nickered in recognition.

"Been cooped up for too long, haven't you?" Fargo asked the black-and-white horse quietly. He ran a comforting hand down the horse's neck. "You'll get plenty of exercise tonight."

The horse didn't say much, just laid his ears back and swiveled an eye at him. The Ovaro had never let him down, and tonight wouldn't be the exception, despite a couple of days in a stall.

Fargo got him saddled and bridled, then led him by the reins out into the street. Sunrise was maybe an hour away at most. Already the sky to the east was more gray than black. He climbed into the saddle and put his spurs to the Ovaro, who broke into a fast trot, anxious to be moving again.

Everything was coming to a head now, and the trail that had originally led to the Blue Emporium and Hattie Hamilton had changed course. Fargo expected to find Hattie, Parker and his men, H.D., Horn or Mc-Kenna or whatever his name was, and, with any luck, Mary, all holed up at Parker's mansion. They would be expecting him, but probably not this morning. It had been a long night and he had considered getting some rest first, but the element of surprise would be a powerful ally.

Clattering over the cobblestones, the rough outlines of a plan began to fall into place. It was early and whatever guards Parker had in place would be tired, maybe even dozing at their posts, waiting for the sun to rise and their chance to bunk down.

The cobblestones gave way to hard-packed dirt, and when Parker's mansion came into view in the distance, Fargo pulled up the Ovaro. The sun was just beginning to rise, silhouetting the main house, and leaving him safely in the shadows.

It was a big place, three stories, with a large wrought-iron fence surrounding it. He couldn't make out the gate—it was still in shadows—but it was a safe bet that it was shut and probably locked. On the rooftop, two men leaned against chimneys, looking like statues. It was another good bet that there were at least a couple of men on the ground as well.

Since surprise was all he had, Fargo decided to use it. "Let's go," he whispered to the Ovaro, who tossed his head in agreement. It occurred to him that if half the men he'd known were as game as his horse, a lot of the fights in his life would have gone differently.

He touched his spurs behind the girth strap, asking the horse for more speed. Little by little, he encouraged the Ovaro to go faster, so that by the time they were twenty yards from the front gate, they were moving at almost a full gallop.

Trusting the horse to know its job, Fargo looped the reins loosely over the saddle horn, and pulled his Henry from the saddle boot. He didn't waste time, but simply sighted on the gate's lock and fired. The sound was horrendously loud in the early-morning quiet, but he saw the metal splinter under the impact. The two statues on the roof jolted to life, looking around in a panic for the source of the gunfire.

Fargo didn't give them time to think too hard on it. As they ran to the edge of the roof and looked down, he signaled the Ovaro to stop, raised the Henry once more, and fired twice. One man clutched at his chest and fell from the roof with a wordless cry.

He missed the second, but the shot was enough to drive him back from the edge of the roof and take cover, which was all Fargo needed. He nudged the horse once more and pushed through the front gate. Two more men were running toward the front of the house, darker shadows on the ground. Fargo slid the Henry back into the boot and pulled his Colt.

He sighted on the closer of the two and fired twice. The man pitched over backward, screaming in pain. By then, the second man had closed the distance and he reached up to grab the Ovaro's reins. Why he didn't pull his gun, Fargo would never know, because two things happened at once: the horse whipped his head around and bit the man in the fleshy part of his arm, and Fargo used the butt end of the Colt to split his skull.

The man slumped to the ground, unconscious or dead. Fargo didn't care which, so long as he was out of the action.

He spurred the Ovaro forward, heading for the front door. The man on the roof took a couple of wild shots, but he'd misjudged Fargo's position and they missed by a good ways. He reached the front door, then jumped out of the saddle.

"No use knocking," he said, and lashed out with one strong kick. The door flew open, hitting the man standing behind it in the nose and breaking it with a faint crunching sound. The man let out a yell and Fargo stepped through, whipping his body around the door.

Holding his nose with one hand, the man was raising his gun with the other.

Once again, Fargo's Colt barked and the man was shoved back into the wall, leaving a bloody red trail down the plaster. The bullet had passed through his chest and he was dead before he hit the floor, his eyes full of surprise.

Fargo paused to listen, trying to determine where the others might be. This floor sounded quiet, but above his head, floorboards creaked softly. He moved for the stairs, reloading the Colt as he did so.

At the top of the stairs, a hallway split left and right. Another flight of stairs continued up to the third floor, but he was fairly certain that those rooms would be for Parker's men and staff. He stopped once more to listen, then moved down the hall to the right. Four doors, two on each side of the hallway, and an open door at the end which showed a washroom that was empty.

To the left, there were only two doors, one on each side of the hall, and a larger set of double doors at the end of the hall. Parker's room, no doubt. From above, he could hear the sound of booted steps. The man on the roof had decided to come inside.

Fargo didn't want anyone sneaking up behind him, so he changed direction, and quietly positioned himself on the stairs. He pushed his hat down over his face and left his right arm outstretched, fingers loosely clasped around the butt of his Colt. His legs he left at awkward angles.

The man, who was now coming down the stairs, would hopefully think that he was dead, shot by the inside guard while he was going up the stairs. A moment of confusion would be all that was needed. Several more steps and Fargo could hear the man's rapid breath. He was nervous and scared, then he saw Fargo's body and let out a sigh of relief.

"Zeke!" he hissed. "Zeke, you got him!"

He took another few steps and now Fargo could see the tips of his boots on the same step where his head rested.

"Zeke, where the hell are you?" the man called. "You got him."

He bent down to remove Fargo's hat, and Fargo sprang like a coiled rattlesnake.

"Oh, shit," the man had time to say. He saw Fargo's mortuary smile, and then nothing as the Colt did its work. The shot was somewhat muffled in the man's coat, but the echo was still explosively loud in the close confines of the stairwell.

The guard grunted as the bullet hit his stomach and exited through his back, shattering his spine. For a long moment, he simply stood there, gasping, his eyes wide and his hands clutching at the lapels of Fargo's coat, then he toppled sideways, rolling down the stairs.

Moving quickly, Fargo returned to the second-floor hallway, and went left. He paused at the first door and listened. Hushed voices could be heard through the wood.

"Maybe he got him," Fargo heard Parker say. "Go take a look, H.D."

"Don't be a fool," H.D. replied. "If you're so certain, *you* go take a look."

"Both of you shut up," Hattie snapped.

Fargo considered the situation. There were at least two, probably three or more guns in there. He couldn't exclude Hattie by reason of her being a woman. Especially considering that it was more than likely that she had killed Beares.

And that still left Horn or McKenna unaccounted for.

Still, Fargo guessed that fear and optimism were his best allies. He knocked lightly on the door. "He's dead, boss," he said, trying to keep his voice gruff.

"Oh, thank God," Parker exclaimed, his voice much louder. "I told you my men could handle him."

Fargo stepped away from the door and to one side. He heard the footsteps coming, then the door opened and Parker stepped out. "Where the hell—"

Fargo put the Colt against the back of his head and cocked it.

"Hell just about sums it up, doesn't it, Senator?"

Fargo said from behind him. "In fact, that's probably where you're headed next."

Parker's hands shot into the air. "Don't shoot me, Fargo, please."

Fargo was about to say more when a shot rang out from inside the room. The bullet caught Parker directly in the temple, spraying blood, bone, and brain matter across the narrow hallway. He dropped dead.

Knowing that hesitation would be just as likely to get him killed, Fargo tore open the door and lunged into the room, falling into a roll, but keeping a firm grip on his Colt.

Hattie held a Colt .45 in her hands, the barrel still smoking.

"Hattie, what the hell did you do!" H.D. exclaimed.

"Solved a problem," she said, her voice ice-cold.

Fargo came to his feet, keeping his gun trained on them. "Nobody moves," he said.

"You truly are dumb, Fargo," Hattie snapped. "If you shoot me, H.D. will gun you down. If you shoot him, I'll gun you down. You're not that fast."

Fargo's lake blue eyes narrowed slightly and he grinned. "Are you willing to bet your life on it?" he asked.

Suddenly, H.D. pulled his own piece and put it to Hattie's head. "Hattie Hamilton," he said, his voice shaking. "You're under arrest."

"What?" she screeched, turning away from Fargo, turning the gun toward H.D.

"Ah, damn," Fargo muttered, then shot her in the arm.

She screamed and dropped the gun, which H.D. quickly picked up.

"You sonsabitches," she moaned, holding her arm. "You goddamn sonsabitches."

Fargo looked at H.D. "What's it going to be, old friend?" he asked. "Do I have to kill you?"

H.D. slowly lowered his own gun, putting it back in the holster, and tossed Hattie's across the room. "I wish you wouldn't, Fargo. At least not until I can explain."

A voice from the doorway said, "I may be able to help with that."

Fargo turned to see Horn standing in the doorway, a grin on his face. "The least you can do, Fargo, is say you're sorry for hitting me in the head."

"Who are you really?" Fargo snapped.

"I tried to tell you," the man said. "I'm James McKenna, of the Pinkerton Agency."

"So what's your role in this, H.D.?" Fargo asked. "I thought you were in it with Hattie and the others."

H.D. nodded, then knelt down and tore a strip of sheet off the bed, using it to bind the still-cursing woman's bleeding arm.

"I've been working with the Pinkertons," H.D. said. "It's a long story, but I had to make everyone think that I was on the take. It was the only way to get close enough to find out what Parker and Beares were really up to."

Fargo looked at the two men, then nodded and holstered his Colt. "What now?" he asked. "Aside from needing a drink and an explanation, I've had about all of New Orleans I can stand."

"Let's get Miss Hamilton here to the sawbones," H.D. replied. "Then we'll explain everything."

"Do I have your word on that?" Fargo asked.

His old friend nodded. "This time, it's the truth, the whole truth, and nothing but. You have my word."

"Then let's go," Fargo said. "I just have one more thing to do."

"What's that?" McKenna asked.

Fargo stepped into the hall and rolled Parker's body over. Inside his suit coat, he found the man's wallet and pulled a stack of bills from it. "Just collecting my paycheck," he said. "After all, no one cheated at the poker game and that's what he paid me for."

McKenna laughed. "You're something of a mercenary, aren't you, Fargo?"

Fargo gave McKenna a warning glance. "I wouldn't

push that if I were you. Now, where's Mary?" he asked. "I thought for sure you'd killed her or something."

"Not at all," McKenna said. "She's safely tucked away over by the sheriff's office. We've got two deputies keeping an eye on her."

Relieved, Fargo helped them gather Hattie Hamilton off the floor, then they escorted her out the door and headed back into New Orleans and the Storyville district.

There were still answers he wanted, but as far as Fargo was concerned, this game was almost played out.

14

The morning sun was bright and quickly burning off the mist that drifted in from the swamps and the shore during the long hours of the night. New Orleans was waking up, a slumbering two-bit whore rising from her filthy mattress to greet another day.

Fargo's eyes scanned the buildings and the people as he and the others rode by, heading into Storyville to bring an end to things. The Ovaro nickered and huffed several times, obviously not pleased to be riding back into the city. He was an animal that, like his owner, much preferred the open trail.

Looking around, Fargo realized that they were in a section of the city he hadn't seen before. The buildings seemed to symbolize the things he didn't like about the city itself. They were either mausoleumlike tombs or crowded together and dirty. It was little wonder that fires had ravaged them so often. From what he could see, many of the buildings were still stained with grime and soot. There was little in this place that appealed to him.

With H.D. in front of him, holding Hattie on his saddle, and McKenna behind him, Fargo figured not too many people would bother to stop them and he was right. Most of the people they passed simply glanced and looked away. A few stared, but they were the stares of the terminally curious—the people who would watch a hanging for entertainment simply because it was there.

They rode down the center of Basin Street and went past Anderson's Café, which was still closed. Fargo reckoned that the man had decided to hunker down until the situation settled. It proved that he was a lot smarter than your average street criminal. He'd built himself a little empire and he sensed that a great burning was about to come. He wanted to hold on to his dream a while longer and Fargo couldn't blame him.

If what McKenna had told him was true, New Orleans would burn again—a fiery death to serve as an example for the rest of the country. It seemed pointless to Fargo, but how could he stop it? Killing McKenna would only get the Pinkerton Agency on his trail and they'd send other agents down here to do their hideous deed, anyway.

He sighed heavily, and felt the first waves of genuine exhaustion wash over him. He wanted a meal, a drink, and a long bit of sleep. Then he wanted out of this place as fast as his Ovaro could take him. He'd collected a good bit of money—though not as much as he'd hoped—but still more than enough to keep him in steak and good sour mash for a long while to come.

They pulled up their horses outside H.D.'s office and tied them to the rail. H.D. climbed out of the saddle, then assisted Hattie down as well. McKenna tied his own horse while Fargo eased out of his own saddle. He was bone-tired.

"Come on inside," H.D. said. "I'll brew us up a pot of coffee."

"Sounds fine," Fargo said. "What about her?"

"McKenna, would you mind going down to the sawbones' office—it's just down the street—and bringing him back here to patch her up? We need to keep her here."

"Sure," he said. He touched a hand gingerly to his scalp and winced. "Maybe he can look at this knot on my head, too. You hit hard, Trailsman."

"I've been told that before," Fargo said. He followed H.D. into the sheriff's office and took a seat while H.D. put Hattie in a holding cell.

She screeched like a banshee until H.D. snapped at

her to shut up or she could damn well do without the doctor, too. She shut up, which Fargo was grateful for.

H.D. got the coffee brewing and by the time it had started to percolate, McKenna came back, dragging the doctor along, who wasn't very happy at being rousted from his office. He was an older man, with a stout build and a shock of white hair. His face was wide and heavily jowled, and his skin was so pale he almost looked like a ghost.

"I had to threaten to arrest him," McKenna said. "Says he doesn't do house calls anymore."

"This isn't a house, Dr. Jennings," H.D. snarled. "It's a jail, and when I call for you, I expect you to move your ass on down here."

"For God's sake, H.D., it's not even office hours," Jennings said. "What's so . . ." His voice trailed off into silence as he caught sight of Hattie in the cell. "You shot Hattie Hamilton?"

"No, I did," Fargo said.

"So how come she's in the cell and you're not?" Jennings asked.

"*That,*" McKenna interrupted, "is none of your damn business."

"Huh," the doctor said. He turned back to H.D. "Well, if you want her patched up, you're going to have to let me in there."

H.D. opened the cell and Jennings got to work. He unwrapped the makeshift bandage and examined the wound. "It's pretty clean," he said. "Went right through and doesn't look like any of the bones are broken." He began applying alcohol liberally and Hattie hissed in pain. "Could've been a lot worse, Miss Hamilton," he said.

"Yeah," Fargo said. "I could have shot her in the nethers and put her out of business for good."

The men chuckled and Hattie just stared hatefully at them. H.D. fished out some mostly clean coffee cups and poured out three cups of black coffee. "I don't use chicory," he said. "But this is some kind of bean the French like."

145

Fargo took a sip of his and his eyebrows went up in surprise. The flavor was dark and rich, and the coffee was thick enough to almost have a texture. "That's different," he said. "But very good."

The men waited silently until Dr. Jennings was finished and had Hattie's arm bandaged up. "Change the bandage once a day, and try to keep it still for a few days," he admonished her as he finished tying the sling. "And don't get it wet. I'll come check on you again in a week and see how you're doing."

He stepped out of her cell, shutting the door behind him, and stopped at H.D.'s desk. "You want me to bill the county for this, H.D.?"

"Just like any other prisoner," H.D. replied. "Thanks for coming."

"Not a problem," Jennings said. "So long as I get paid."

"Don't you always?" H.D. snapped. "It's all about the payday for you, isn't it, Doc?"

"You're no different," the doctor said, then turned and stamped out of the office.

"It's going to take me years to repair my reputation, McKenna," H.D. said. "Years."

"I think with what you'll earn from the agency, you might consider an early retirement," McKenna replied. "Or maybe starting over somewhere new."

"Maybe," H.D. said.

Fargo cleared his throat. "Gents, I am plumb exhausted and I'm still waiting for an explanation."

H.D. nodded. "Sure, Fargo. You're right. McKenna, why don't you start?"

"Okay," McKenna said. He eased back in his chair and turned his gaze on Fargo. "Like I told you last night, I work for the Pinkerton agency. What I couldn't tell you was that H.D. here was working with us. I was out investigating Horn's death, so I hadn't had a chance to talk to H.D. before the poker game. For all I knew, you were in on the whole thing."

"*What* whole thing?" Fargo asked.

"I'm getting there," the agent replied. "Parker and

Beares were using Storyville as a way to launder and counterfeit money, Fargo. That's why they started hassling Anderson. He owns enough of the businesses in this area that it was cramping their ability to get the money through. They wanted him out, but he was too popular to kill outright."

"But they're senators," Fargo said. "Why not just take bribes or something?"

McKenna laughed. "Oh, there was plenty of that, too, and we don't mind that so much. But when people start laundering illegal money and printing their own, we—or should I say our client, the United States government—takes exception to that."

"So why involve H.D.?"

"I can answer that one," his old friend said. "I wanted to help. McKenna here came to me about six months after I got here, just trying to get the lay of the land. When he told me what he was up to, I asked if I could help."

"And the only way you could do that," Fargo guessed, "was to get inside their organizations."

"Exactly," H.D. said. "What I wasn't expecting was you to show up, working for Parker. I wasn't sure what to do then, except keep going and see how things played out."

"I didn't know what Parker was doing," Fargo said. "He just hired me for the poker game after I caught someone trying to cheat him."

"That's the part," McKenna said, "that still doesn't make sense to me. Why hire someone to catch cheaters, when he planned on cheating himself? And why kill Beares?"

From her cell, Hattie laughed contemptuously. "Because Beares wanted out, you idiots," she said. "He grew himself a conscience and felt like they were making plenty of money."

"So you shot him?" H.D. asked.

"Hell, no," she said. "Parker did. Then he handed me the gun before any of you got there. I just played along."

"So why'd you shoot Parker, then?" Fargo asked. "If you were in cahoots with him, and he was using the Blue Emporium for so many of his deals, why kill him?"

Hattie laughed again, and Fargo felt a chill run down his spine. This was a woman with no compassion at all. "Because I've made enough money, too," she said, her voice like a block of ice. "He was starting to want more from me than I was willing to give and his demands were unreasonable. I got what I wanted from him."

"You are one cold bitch," McKenna said.

"Yes, I am," she replied. "But I'm now a *rich* cold bitch."

"You're also in jail," he reminded her.

"But she's not staying," Fargo said. "Is she, H.D.?"

"No," he said, his voice filled with sadness. "I'm going to cut her loose."

"What?" McKenna asked. "Why? She *killed* a man, H.D."

"It was part of the deal," he said. "Without Hattie's help, I would never have gained access to Parker and Beares."

"There's more," Fargo said. "I can hear it in your voice."

He nodded. "You don't have to make me say it, Fargo," he said. "What's the point?"

"There isn't one, but McKenna needs to hear it."

"Fine," his old friend snapped. "She's going free because I . . . I love her," he admitted. "She's cold and ruthless and a user, but . . . when I'm with her, she makes me feel alive again."

McKenna shook his head. "It's your choice, of course. We don't need her for Parker and Beares. Between the evidence at their mansions and what we've gotten the last few weeks, they'll be found guilty after death and their possessions auctioned off to pay restitution."

Political corruption, Fargo realized, wasn't all that different from the other kinds of moneygrubbing he'd seen in the West. Even the rich wanted to be richer. "Why'd you tell me that the Pinkertons were going to burn down New Orleans?" he asked McKenna. "Why not just tell me the truth?"

McKenna chuckled. "I still hadn't spoken to H.D. and you were working for Parker. I figured that the worst case would be that you'd run to Parker with the story and maybe he'd back down. I didn't count on you hitting me in the head and dragging me off to jail."

"Well, if we cross paths again, you'll know for next time," Fargo said. He stood up, stretched, and put his empty coffee cup on the desk. "I guess that's about it for me. I'm going to get some food and some sleep."

H.D. nodded. "I'm sorry about what happened here, Fargo. If I could've told you the truth sooner, I would have."

"I'm just glad you hadn't really crossed the line," he replied. "I would've killed you, H.D. Bad men are bad enough, but good men who've gone bad . . . they're worse than rabid dogs."

"I know," he said. "I'll get Hattie back over to her place and then I'll send Mary over to the Bayou. She should be there before long."

"Fine," Fargo said. "Just make sure she steers clear of Hattie. You may love her, but I know a black widow when I see one."

"There's no accounting for love, is there, Fargo?" H.D. asked. "It just shows up when it wants to."

Fargo was silent for a long minute; then he said, "I wouldn't know. I can talk about death and fighting and horses and a lot of other things, but love and I don't cross trails too often."

"You're a hard man, Fargo," he said. "But sooner or later, it will catch up to you, too."

Fargo grinned. "Not if I ride fast enough, it won't."

He started to step out the door, but McKenna's voice stopped him short. "There's just one more thing before you go," he said.

Fargo turned back to the Pinkerton man. "What's that?"

"The money," McKenna said. "What did you do with it?"

"I gave it to a politician," he said. "The mayor of Storyville."

"That's . . . that's evidence, Fargo," McKenna said. "We need to get that back."

"Sounds like a real problem," he said. "He'll probably make some kind of deal for it. Perhaps a promise of no Pinkerton involvement in Storyville for a long, long time. Or maybe cash."

"Anderson's barely more than a common criminal!" McKenna objected. "Why should we deal with him?"

Hattie's voice, tired out now from crying, said, "Because he cares, the dumb sonofabitch. He keeps this place running, and he practically built Basin Street. Without him, the real criminals will run the place." She cackled softly. "You need him if you don't want this place to really come apart at the seams."

"Makes sense to me," Fargo said. He tipped his hat to them, then stepped out into the morning sunshine, grateful to be away.

He didn't think he'd ever really trust H.D. again, but he didn't have to. It was a big country and this piece of it was one that he didn't want to visit ever again.

Let the schemers have it, he thought. *I'd rather be in the West.* Out there he understood the people and the land, and more importantly, he felt at ease with himself. The trail that had led him here had taught him one thing: the trails in the city are just as bloody and dangerous as those on the frontier.

The only difference, he noted as he patted the wad of cash in his vest, was that the paychecks were sometimes bigger. But money wasn't everything, and he had all he really needed with his Colt, his Henry, his Ovaro . . . and his burning desire to live free.

By the time he'd stabled the Ovaro and made his way back to the diner next door to the Bayou, Fargo was all but asleep on his feet. Still, he needed food first. He hadn't eaten in a couple of days and the rich coffee H.D. had given him was sitting in his stomach like a lead weight.

He pushed open the door of the diner and found a seat at the counter, nodding at the man who came over to take his order.

"If you don't mind me saying so, you look done in," he said.

"I just about am," Fargo admitted. "But I could use a bite to eat before I get some sleep. What've you got?"

The man smiled, his teeth so white against his black skin that they were almost blinding. "I've got just the thing, sir. Scrambled eggs, spicy French sausage, and fried potatoes with peppers and onions wrapped up together in a nice soft tortilla." He paused, then said, "It's a little bit . . ."

"Spicy," Fargo finished for him. "The last time I was told that here, my tongue almost fell out." He took off his hat and set it on the counter. "Sounds perfect."

"Yes, sir," the man said, jotting a note on his pad and heading back to the kitchen.

Fargo helped himself to the pot of coffee on the counter, and waited patiently for the man to return with his meal. It only took a few minutes for the man to appear with a platter heaped with three of the tortilla concoctions and a jar of salsa. "Some folks like to put this on theirs," he said.

"They make something similar in Mexico," Fargo said. "Huevos rancheros."

"Eat," the man said. "Then we'll see how our food stacks up against the Mexicans'."

Fargo slathered the salsa inside one of the tortillas, closed it back up, and took a big bite. There was some kind of cheese in addition to all the other ingredients, and the taste was phenomenal. "Mmm . . ." he said, chewing and swallowing the bite. "That's good."

Then the spices hit, and Fargo felt the blood drain

from his face. A wave of heat, and then the blood all came rushing back. "Wahhh . . ." he managed, reaching for the glass of water the man was holding out in his hand. He took several large swallows, then tore off a piece of the tortilla and ate that, too. "Good God," he said. "That's . . . it sort of sneaks up on a man, doesn't it?"

The server smiled his big white grin and said, "It sure does, sir. You enjoy your breakfast." Then he moved off down the counter to serve other customers. Fargo assumed the man stayed close by for the first bite for the entertainment value . . . or maybe to save someone's life if the heat was too much and they collapsed. His tongue was still burning.

But they were damn good tortillas. He dove back in, drinking copious amounts of water to keep the heat to a manageable level. When he was full, he sat back with a satisfied sigh and pushed his plate away.

The man came by, still grinning, and took it away, then refilled Fargo's coffee.

Fargo wasn't sure where he'd go from here. The only thing he knew was that he planned on leaving New Orleans and riding west.

The server said, "You seem kind of restless."

"It shows, huh?" Fargo smiled.

"Got a brother like that. Can't stay in one place more than a month or so. Always looking for the big dream to come true."

"Think it ever will?"

"I doubt it." He smiled. "But I don't think that matters to him. It's the looking he likes. The wandering. I get the sense you're a lot like that yourself."

"I guess I've done some of that wandering from time to time."

"Looking for the big dream to come true?"

He shrugged. "Not that so much. It's just that I like to see what's over the next hill, I guess."

He laughed softly. "Yep, peas in a pod. You and my brother."

Fargo tossed some money on the counter, settled

his hat on his head, and left the diner. He was still tired, but he felt better for having eaten. Now what he really wanted was a good long nap.

As he looked around at the people and the buildings, he realized that even a town he disliked as much as this one could probably become home for him if he stayed long enough. A person could get used to just about anything if he gave it enough time. He supposed that most of the good, hardworking people here managed to get used to the corruption and the violence. They just went on with their daily lives and hoped it didn't touch on them or their loved ones.

The Bayou was quiet and the clerk nodded politely to him as he passed by the desk, saying, "We fixed your door."

"Appreciate it."

"Mr. Fargo—" The clerk wanted to say more but it was probably only clerk babble as far as Fargo was concerned. He walked over to the stairs. All he wanted was some rest. Time for clerk chatter when he checked out.

Something felt funny as he approached his door. He paused in the hallway. Listened. But nothing but silence filled his ears. Still and all he sensed something wrong. He'd developed survival instincts over the years that could pick up on the slightest threat.

And he found that his sense of danger was correct.

His door was open a crack. Could one of Parker's or Beares' men still be wandering around looking for revenge? He didn't know, but he pulled the Colt from the holster and eased up to his door to listen.

The room was quiet. He used the barrel of the gun to push the door open even more. The door cried a bit as it opened. Hinges needed some oil. He took a single step forward. And then another step.

Given the small size of the room, it was easy to scan. Easy to spot any kind of threat. He kept his Colt clenched tight in his hand.

Then he smiled. Guess he wouldn't be needing his

Colt after all. The room was empty . . . except for the slender figure on the bed, where Mary was curled up on the blankets, a chocolate ribbon of silk, sound asleep. She hadn't even heard him come in.

Fargo turned and quietly shut and locked the door, then hung his hat and his gun belt on the dresser. He didn't want to disturb her, so he took his boots off standing up, then removed the rest of his clothing and tiptoed to the other side of the bed.

It was far too hot and humid in New Orleans to sleep under the blankets, so he contented himself with sliding down next to her, and wrapping her in his arms. She murmured softly in her sleep and he planted a warm kiss on her neck.

He felt her beginning to respond to him and so he whispered in her ear, "Mary, it's Fargo."

She arched her back against him and in the sexiest voice he'd ever heard said, "I knew it. I knew you'd be safe, Skye. I prayed for you, too."

"I didn't know what happened to you," he said.

"I'm fine," she whispered. "Just fine." She rolled over and planted a very warm, soft kiss on his lips. "But I'd be a whole lot finer if you made love to me, Skye."

He placed his hands on either side of her face. "Mary, you know I can't stay here, right? You know I'm moving on?"

Her eyes were dark and serious, then she nodded. "I know, Skye. You aren't the kind of man to stay around. But I'd . . . can you make me feel safe for just one more day? I know it's just pretend, but can you make love to me like we did out at the grotto?"

His hands found her breasts and his lips pressed forward on hers. Suddenly, he knew that at least some of his money would go to buy a better life for her. Maybe get her started on a little place of her own somewhere. She could learn about horses and cattle.

"Yes," she moaned into his ear as he gently squeezed her nipples. "Just like that, Skye." She opened her legs to him, shifting her hips so that he

154

could enter her. Things moved quickly and soon she was climaxing beneath him, shuddering and moaning. They continued their lovemaking until they were both exhausted, and Mary fell asleep, curled up once more in his arms, feeling safer, no doubt, than she ever had in her life.

Fargo drifted into a light doze himself, thinking that tomorrow he would ride west and see what the frontier might bring him.

*Oregon, 1860—where Skye Fargo follows
a trail of gun smoke and dead men to clear
his name.*

The big man in buckskins leaned against the wall near
the closed door of the barn, which smelled of manure,
moldy hay, and the tobacco smoke that drifted in
thready clouds. The whole place hummed with the
talk of the men gathered around the cockpit, a makeshift ring formed by rough boards.

Around half of the pit was a makeshift grandstand
to accommodate those who wanted a close look at the
fight that was about to begin. Those who hadn't arrived early enough to get a seat had to stand around
the other part of the pit, and there was plenty of pushing and shoving for position.

Skye Fargo's lake blue eyes watched as the men jos-
tled one another and crowded closer to the ring. Some
of them were well dressed, a banker or two, and maybe a
lawyer. Others wore rough work clothes that hadn't
been washed in a while. According to Dodge Calder,
Fargo's friend, one of them was the town marshal.

Fargo didn't look like any of them. His fringed buckskins seemed a little out of place, and it was clear that he was accustomed to being outside in the open, not closed up in a building like the bankers.

Only a couple of women were present, both of them soiled doves from some local saloon, Fargo figured. Their faces were avid with anticipation, and it was likely that they'd make a good bit of money from the customers who'd be eager for their favors later, after their blood had been stirred by the fight to the death between two roosters.

Money changed hands and bets went down. Fargo heard an occasional nervous laugh, indicating that some of the bettors were a little unsure they'd made the right choice.

On one side of the ring a man with a corncob pipe clamped between his teeth watched as another man took the hood off the orange-colored head of a fighting cock with its comb and wattles trimmed so that its opponent in the coming battle couldn't grab them with its bill.

The man with the pipe removed it from his mouth and breathed a cloud of smoke into the cock's face to agitate it, not that it didn't appear agitated enough already.

Both men wore ragged shirts and denim pants that showed hard use. Lank hair hung down from their sweat-stained hats.

On the other side of the pit, the handler of the opposing cock spoke soothingly to it and almost seemed to cuddle it as he checked on the short, sharp metal spurs affixed to its legs where its own spurs would have been. Fargo couldn't make out the handler's eyes because they were hidden by a hat pulled down low on the forehead so that the features were obscured.

"That kid's been braggin' about how many fights that big black bird's won," Dodge Calder said. He took off a battered hat and ran skinny fingers through his thick white whiskers. "You might wanna make a bet on that cock. Name's Satan."

The kid's rooster was so black that it was almost purple. It stretched its long neck toward its handler as if listening carefully to what was being said. Its wattles and comb had been trimmed like the other bird's.

"I don't bet on things I don't know much about," Fargo told Calder.

Calder nodded. "Don't blame you. The Bryson brothers don't lose often."

Fargo had known Calder for a long time, and in fact he'd stopped off in Ashland to see him after leading some pilgrims up the Applegate Trail to the Willamette Valley. Calder had been a guide for a few years, which is how Fargo had gotten to know him, but Calder had liked Oregon so much that one year he'd decided to stay and see if there was any gold left in the area that some of the forty-niners had drifted to when the pickings got slim in California.

As far as the Trailsman knew, Calder hadn't found any gold, but he'd found himself a home in Ashland, a little farther to the south of the gold fields. He'd done some trading and trapping and was making a living for himself one way and another.

Fargo was happy for Calder, but he wasn't interested in settling down in one spot, no matter how easy it might be to make a living there. He was a natural wanderer, not cut out to be tied to one place for any length of time.

There wasn't a lot to do in Ashland, and Calder had suggested the cockfight as a bit of entertainment on a Sunday afternoon. Fargo didn't see much amusement in a couple of roosters trying to kill each other, but Calder wanted to get a bet down.

"I got my money on the Brysons," he told Fargo. "The kid's been lucky, but those old boys have been at this a long time, and they don't like to lose. That rooster of theirs is rough as a cob. They call him General Washington, and he's won four fights in a row. Fact is, nobody around here will fight against him. That's why we got such a good crowd. Folks wouldn't turn out like this to see just an ordinary fight."

Satan against General Washington, Fargo thought. If the birds lived up to their names it would be quite a fight.

Fargo was about to say something along those lines to Calder, but someone moved a board aside and the referee stepped into the ring. He was the man Fargo thought might have been a lawyer. He walked to the middle of the ring and took a thick watch out of the pocket of his black frock coat. The crowd grew quiet.

"One round of thirty minutes is what we've agreed on, gentlemen," the referee said. "Is that correct?"

The Bryson brothers, who didn't look like any gentlemen Fargo had ever seen before, nodded.

"Or till our rooster kills that one," one of the brothers said.

The other brother grinned. The kid ignored them.

"Very well," the referee said. He backed up a little. "Bill your birds."

When he said that, one of the Brysons nodded to his brother and stepped out of the ring.

"That's Hap," Calder said. "He's the cheerful one."

Hap didn't look cheerful to Fargo. He looked mean as a cornered cougar.

"The other one's Willie," Calder said.

Willie looked just like Hap to Fargo. As far as he could tell, they might have been twins.

Willie took General Washington to the middle of the ring, holding the cock's legs together with its body draped over his left arm. The kid walked up to him, holding Satan the same way. They let the two birds glare at each other, keeping them a foot or so apart. The birds squirmed for a couple of seconds as if trying to escape, but their handlers gripped them tightly. When the gamecocks saw they couldn't get free, they started to stretch their necks and peck at each other, trying to reach an eye or some other soft spot. Their handlers pulled them back before they could make any contact.

The sparring went on for a short time, maybe half a minute. Fargo didn't see much point to it. The birds already hated each other plenty. They didn't need any encouragement.

"That's enough," the referee said. "Get ready."

The handlers backed away from the center of the ring and squatted down with eight or nine feet of empty space between them.

"Pit your birds!" the referee called out, and as he did the handlers released the cocks. The quiet exploded in a flurry of feathers. The spectators pressed around the ring. They yelled, shoved each other, and made more bets.

What happened between the cocks was almost too fast for Fargo to follow. The kid's bird flapped its clipped wings and seemed to go straight into the air as if on a spring and then to descend on General Washington before the cock had a chance to gain any height. After that, the birds attacked each other, heads darting, feet scrambling, spurs flashing.

Fargo thought that if he'd been more used to cockfights, he'd have been able to follow what was happening better, but because he didn't know what to watch for, the subtleties, if any, were lost on him.

General Washington, however, was getting the worst of it. Fargo could see that much. Satan was pecking furiously at the general's head from his superior position, trying to get at the eyes, but the general was strong and somehow got out from under his opponent and scuttled away to the side. The kid's rooster backed away a short distance, the clipped tips of his outstretched wings quivering.

The two birds glared at each other for a couple of seconds like human fighters might as each took his opponent's measure. Then they rushed forward and launched themselves into the air.

This time General Washington got off to a good start, as did Satan, and the birds smacked together a couple of feet above the ground, their wings working rapidly. Their feet kicked so fast that they were just a blur, but neither bird could land a solid blow with either spurs or beak.

Before they fell to the ground, Satan pulled out a couple of the general's feathers, and a few drops of blood hit the dirt of the barn floor as the feathers floated down.

The crowd got rowdier. Most of the men were yelling encouragement at one bird or the other and slapping each other on the back. Even Calder, a man Fargo didn't consider excitable, jumped up and down as he strained to see over the heads of the men in front of him.

The birds rushed together again. Fargo thought they must have been tiring because they didn't gain much altitude. The pecking was just as furious as before, though, and Satan ripped out quite a few more of the general's feathers.

Fargo glanced at the Brysons. They stood stiffly at the side of the ring, stony silent, arms crossed, eyes narrowed. The kid, on the other hand, sat leaning against the boards, to all appearances as calm and relaxed as if sitting in church with a clean conscience.

The fighting cocks clashed again, this time without rising from the ground. Satan got his beak into General Washington's neck and twisted. The birds fell to the ground, and Satan flapped his wings to rise above the General. He hacked at the general with his spurs, slashing at his eyes.

The General's neck writhed as the bird tried to avoid the stabbing spurs, but one of them sank into his left eye. The General jerked his head away. Blood spurted, and the General went into a frenzied backward dance, his legs hardly touching the ground as he spun and flipped. He fell on his back in the dirt, his wildly beating wings stirring up a small gray storm.

Then he stopped and was still. Satan walked over to the dead bird and hopped onto the body. He looked around the ring slowly and crowed.

Hap Bryson jumped into the ring, his face twisted with rage. Before anyone could stop him, he reached the birds and gave Satan a vicious kick, sending him flying from General Washington's body.

The referee ran toward Bryson. "Stop it, Hap! Get out of the ring!"

Hap either didn't hear him or didn't give a damn. His hand reached for the pistol at his side, and he jerked the gun from its holster.

The kid jumped up and ran toward Hap, but he was too late. The revolver in Hap's hand roared. Satan exploded in a bloody mass of feathers.

The kid landed on Hap's back, fingers tearing wildly at his eyes. Fargo thought for a second that Hap might meet the same fate as General Washington.

Willie Bryson must have thought the same thing because he leaped to his brother's aid. He had a wide-bladed knife in his hand. He crossed the pit with a couple of long strides, and raised the knife to strike at the kid's back.

At that point things started to go to hell.

No other series packs this much heat!

THE TRAILSMAN

National Bestselling Author
RALPH COMPTON